THE CHOCOLATE DEAL

THE CHOCOLATE DEAL

A NOVEL

HAIM GOURI

Translated by Seymour Simckes
Foreword by Geoffrey Hartman

Wayne State University Press

Original Hebrew edition copyright © 1965 by Haim Gouri.
English translation copyright © 1968 by Haim Gouri.
Foreword copyright © 1999 by Wayne State University Press,
Detroit, Michigan 48201. All rights are reserved.
No part of this book may be reproduced without formal permission.
Manufactured in the United States of America.

03 02 01 00 99   5 4 3 2 1

Library of Congress Cataloging—in—Publication Data

Gouri, Haim, 1923–
    [' Iskat ha-shokolad. English]
    The chocolate deal / Haim Gouri ; translated by Seymour
Simckes ; foreword by Geoffrey Hartman.
    p.   cm.
    Previously published: New York : Holt, Rinehart, and Winston,
1968.
    ISBN 0-8143-2800-8 (pbk: alk. paper)
    I. Simckes, Seymour. II. Title.
PJ5054.G66I813   1999
892.4'36—dc21   99-13470

Foreword

Geoffrey Hartman

Haim Gouri has often been called the national poet of Israel. Many of his poems are familiar to every young person who has gone through Israeli schools; even outside his country his brief and powerful verses on the Akedah, entitled "Inheritance," are well known. The inheritance referred to is "a knife in the heart" that each new generation exposed to that story—and now to the near death of all European Jewry in the Holocaust—cannot escape feeling. Gouri's reputation is not based alone on the strength of his imagination or on a career as poet, journalist, filmmaker, novelist, and soldier that spans the history of the Jews in modern Israel from their struggle against the British in Palestine through the many wars fought by a small and besieged land since 1948, the date of its Independence. What makes Gouri crucial to Israel and Israeli literature is a conscience that never sleeps. Everything that happens, all the "incidents"

The Chocolate Deal

that take an ever-greater toll—a terrorist attack, soldiers killed in Lebanon, the riots, the deaths of Arabs and Jews, the assassination of political leaders, the internal strife between secular and religious factions—come home to him as to a nerve center.

Two moments in his life proved to be especially significant: his daily coverage of the 1961 Eichmann trial for an Israeli newspaper—articles that were collected the following year as *Facing the Glass Cage: Reporting the Eichmann Trial*—and his experiences of Holocaust survivors during a mission to Europe in 1947. These events inspired not only many poems but also a documentary film trilogy completed in 1983. The 1947 visit is also the basis of *The Chocolate Deal* (1965)—too often called simply a novel. It is, rather, a sustained lyric in prose (and not less realistic because of that) in which fantasy and poetry rise like cream to the top and overcome the more prosaic scam that gives the book its title.

Still relatively neglected in Holocaust literature and testimony is the period immediately after liberation. For the survivors, that time was, in a particular sense, not liberating at all: with the Jewish communities in Europe decimated, and most towns in ruins, the way home was often blocked or extremely painful. Even those lucky enough to make it back to their native country often found an ambiguous reception. Primo Levi's *The Reawakening,* an account of the many months it took for him to return, evokes the travails, both physical and spiritual, of that journey. Despite help from abroad, the DP camps often seemed like a prison. Gouri quotes Judges 17:6 to evoke the chaos in which the displaced persons were forced to exist: "In those days ... every man did that which was right in his own eyes."

The unkindest, the worst affliction, however, was the intense loneliness of the survivors deprived of their families. They knew, or feared, they had no one left, yet they desperately looked for purpose and community. In *The Chocolate Deal* Gouri enters the minds of two such survivors, the last of their families, who wander about aimlessly as they remember the promise of their early years.

It is a novel, then, about a radical form of homelessness. Mordi (Mordecai Neuberg) by chance encounters an old friend, Rubi (Reuben Krauss), in one of those ruined and nameless European cities, and the first part of the story follows their attempt to establish a more intimate contact, to stay together. Before the war, Rubi had been something of a mathematical prodigy, and Mordi had studied the poetry of the troubadours. Mordi lives in the cellar of a convent, a tiny space provided by its

Sisters of Mercy; it is, as he tries to persuade a skeptical Rubi, a real "address."

The nature of the displacement suffered by these strays is conveyed by the author's insight into their psychological quirks, miseries, and exaltations. Rubi daydreams about his relatives as if they had not been deported, about how Attorney Salomon and his family, including their servant girl Gerti, would receive him with warmth and astonishment (and, in Gerti's case, erotic compliance), and about rescuing a girl of ten, daughter of Dr. Karl Hoffman, from a burning house.

There are also less innocent, more terrifying, fantasies. Rubi mocks the Sisters of Mercy, who fulfill their duty in a world where the division of duties has become totally unstable and even reversible. "Others kill, and they have mercy. The day will come when these pale, sad women in black shall rage, attack, slaughter. Then the murderers will hasten to our aid, comfort us, serve us a glass of water and, by our blood-stained beds, cross themselves in silence. For the sake of change. Oh, then will salvation come . . . " If there is comedy in apocalypse, Gouri detects it.

Similarly, Mordi, at least according to Rubi, interprets the latter's heroic rescue of the girl as a betrayal, or a sort of atonement. Rubi tells Dr. Hoffman:

Foreword

"According to my friend Mordi, a false play is when you atone, in one moment, for the long crime against the many."

I'm telling him profound things, isn't that so?—profound and very interesting, because Mordi is speaking from my throat, dear Mordi, my dead comrade. I go on: "Try to understand him. He argues that if I had let your daughter burn . . . I'd have confirmed a certain practice."

That's the first hint.

This is not simply the vagary of a morbid imagination. Rubi is hinting that he knows Dr. Hoffman is a Nazi doctor; he assaults him psychologically prior to soliciting his help for the chocolate deal. However disturbing Rubi's own practice is, and however opportunistic he is in making use of his dead friend, the "organizing" here (to use the camp slang)—the nearly impossible procuring of things by shrewd, often illegal means—shows not only intelligence (confirming, in a perverted way, Rubi's early genius) but also reflects the survivors' moral or imaginative need to incorporate the thoughts, even sometimes the identity, of their dead friends.

The chocolate deal itself takes up only the last quarter of the novel. After learning that the authorities wish to ease the food shortage by unloading on the market surplus military chocolate, Rubi concocts a get-rich-quick scheme. With

Dr. Hoffman's help he will spread a rumor that the chocolate contains a sedative meant to pacify the sexual urges of young soldiers away from home. No one will want to touch it then, especially in a society with a surplus of women. Prices will drop, Rubi will buy the chocolate for nothing, the original report will be denied as erroneous, and the price of the chocolate will rise dramatically.

The last we see of Rubi is in the cemetery, probably mourning for his friend, having promised to honor him with a splendid gold-engraved tombstone from the riches to come. Did the deal come off? We suspect not and consider that everything has been the fantasy of a man determined to be bold and active and to not give up on life. In contrast, Mordi's death, which is never fully explained, is foreshadowed by the opposite tendency to brood rather than to fight and to disappear from the scene: "There's no need for any act at all. All there is to do in this case is nothing. I have no strength to refuse this peace, this great alienation. . . . Any other conduct would force me to attach importance to my actions, and that would be a deliberate, foolish, wicked contribution equal to the huge senselessness all around me."

The vigor of this novel comes from the same source as its difficulty. Gouri chooses an omniscient

Foreword

narrator, but rarely moves into the distance away from the thoughts and troubled vision of the two survivors. Only at the very beginning does he approach them from the outside to evoke their aimless, solitary restlessness. But the solitude is inside them. Though they walk together and exchange words, their minds cannot meld—their imaginations are too different, too strong and isolating. Because Gouri reduces descriptive detail concerning person and place to a minimum, the reader gains almost no external picture of the protagonists. Their inner lives, or imaginary conversations, however, are rendered in such hallucinating detail that realism dissolves into phantasmagoria. It sometimes seems as if Rubi is inventing all the characters he speaks about except for Mordi. And sometimes the poet in Gouri identifies so strongly with his characters' thoughts that we forget who is thinking.

> Many things vanished. The weak beatings of the heart remained. Luckily the sun kept its orbit, magnificently unconcerned. Therefore a few certainties endured, like the winds of heaven: East, West, North, South. Day and night. The seasons of the year. There was, in this, a sort of splendid abundance of mockery. What was left for him to do with the seasons of the year, or the winds of heaven? But the passing of time prompts the feeling of going from here to there. A few graced moments of half-crazed comfort.

The Chocolate Deal

We are surprised by the "him." We had forgotten Mordi and were tempted to yield to the poet as he turns a survivor's condition into the human condition.

As this excerpt shows, Seymour Simckes provides a sensitive and lively translation. *The Chocolate Deal* reminds us sometimes of Beckett, sometimes of Paul Celan's *Conversation in the Mountains;* and in its grasp of the psychology of these survivors, who wander about in a kind of trance, it parallels the intuitions of Aharon Appelfeld. Gouri has produced a remarkable book about a time in which time seemed unreal, without direction, and almost unredeemable.

*L*OOMING LARGER, larger, slowing down, at last the train is here. Is here at last. Now the cars empty and the tarred platform fills, and already there's much lugging of baggage, falling on necks, and hastening to exit gates visible in the distance. Lit up. As before. As always.

He, too, gets off. A small suitcase in his hand. A tall man. Bent a bit. Gray-suited. He remains behind. Is he waiting for someone? Does he have time to spare? Then he turns right and under the giant iron-and-glass vault, cracked here and there, he drifts slowly after those who are rushing, like a solitary rear guard.

He leaves. Stands opposite the sun-soaked square. Shuts his eyes tight. Opens them. His name is not known to any of the passers-by on this street paved with dark stones.

As a rule, names don't show on faces, except for the names of the more or less important. He, however, is not important; though much altered by

The Chocolate Deal

time or by suffering, his face still guards some of its characteristics. For him, therefore, it's possible to carry around a remnant of pride and hope to have some chance of being recognized. He's dressed in cast-off clothes. That he has any others with him is inconceivable. What's hidden in that small suitcase? What could be hidden there?

From his jacket he pulls out a pack of cheap cigarettes,—what else?—and lights one. He stands there like a stranger or a blunderer, quiet amidst the bustle. From his manner it's clear that he is neither unbelievably blissful nor dozing. He seems simply not to have figured out yet where to turn. Among the gray houses, the blossoming trees, the men, their women, the blue paleness of the skies; he exploits his right to consider the different possibilities.

How long is a man like him permitted to stand around, altogether unoccupied, without arousing wonder or suspicion? But this is a metropolis with many troubles. And he's just a lost drop.

Time passes. Unless he's decided to become a statue, a monument, some sort of action, movement, is expected, otherwise he's likely, God forbid, to drop from his standing position, and a circle gather for a few minutes to have a look, humming, spreading, until the stretcher arrives.

He exploits, up to the permissible limit his

privilege to stand there, keep silent, and make up his mind. He turns toward the tobacco-newspaper kiosk by the gray, ruined, beautifully ancient wall just opposite him. Once there, he stocks up on cigarettes and a daily paper. A good sign. Afterward, he turns left and walks and walks and walks through the late morning hours, through the winelike atmosphere. He disappears.

But every once in a while he comes back there. Most likely he's looking for someone. Perhaps the man who didn't wait for him on the platform? Why does he return? What is he up to? As he thumbs through his newspaper, his movements seem to become slower. For the most part he skips the giant headlines of the front page, the main news concerning the fate of the world, and devotes himself to examining closely those endless columns of advertisements, the petite letters of the Lost and Found.

According to the amount of time already spent, and still to be spent, stooping there, quietly reading, the man must find this business interesting.

Look. Right now, for example, he sits on the stone bench. Disturbing no one, wanted by none. An hour goes by. And now another man, with pale gray gabardine coat and hat on, approaches the kiosk and buys a pack of Admiral. He pays. Pulls out a cigarette. Turns left. The man holding the newspaper stops reading. The paper sinks onto his lap. He stares. The other man stops dead. Perplexed by the remote, he freezes, just a minute ... a long while.

He turns around, approaches the one getting up from the stone bench to greet him. He is very pale. He asks in a wisp of a whisper, "Excuse me, are you by any chance Rubi Krauss?"

Before any passers-by sense what's happening, the two unknown men fall upon each other's necks, like two wrestlers of huge strength. Welded together. Forming a twisted sculpture entitled, perhaps, "The Reunion."

"Rubi," sobs the nameless man.

After a silence generations long, the unknown one asks, "Rubi, you're alive?"

And the man called Rubi answers, "You see."

The unnamed man must make sure, confirm appearances, verify this total unlikelihood. Judging by his face, he seems to be dreaming now. He completes a hasty check. He awakens, startled; he takes a tiny step backward. More than that he doesn't permit himself.

Now he examines the man standing opposite him as if he had not seen him for a long time. He knows this himself. He shuts his eyes for a second. Opens them. The man is still standing there. Now he sees another face upon the man before him. But that face also fits his name. And so it *is* him. Apparently it's him. After all.

Even so, passed here by accident. I came over to buy cigarettes; pure luck. He was reading a newspaper. He happened to show his face. I could have walked on. What luck. Such luck. Who would have guessed it. Here. Like this. On a bench. What was he doing here? How did he come to this bench? Interesting. A miracle. My God. I just happened to pass by.

Rubi waits for his friend to return from the long trip.

"How are you?" asks the unnamed man.

"Living," says Rubi.

The train-station clock shows twelve-thirty.

"When did you arrive?"

"About a month ago."

"What are you doing right now?"

"Nothing."

"Let's have a bite to eat."

"Okay, let's have a bite to eat."

They start walking, and this is how they walk. Together. Talking to one another. That one not asking anything before its proper time and this one not giving an answer that may someday become evident of itself.

The Chocolate Deal

"There's a cafeteria not far from here," says the friend.

"I know."

"Have you been in it?"

"I know the place."

When he's had enough of this, the friend says, "I just happened to pass by." Then he adds something like "the finger of God."

"Not a bad cafeteria."

"Yes."

"Kosher."

"Makes no difference."

"Afterward," says the friend to himself, "afterward."

The two enter the small soup kitchen in Bat Alley not far from the statue *The Black Plague*, a thing of beauty and commemoration which stands in the main street of the capital city.

The cafeteria is a big hall full of tables, full of people. It looks like any other cafeteria, yet actually only a few peculiar places can match it: the waiters here know the orders of the customers in advance. So they save themselves the extra movements of going over to ask and coming back to shout into the tiny slot to the kitchen.

A giant pot stands there, gold and blue, solitary and steaming, and by it a red-cheeked girl. Now there begins a one-way traffic, laden with soup and bread, to those waiting in silence, or conversing in whispers. It's unfortunate, but they do not even notice the noble, slender, extended, towerlike form of the wine bottles on the snow-white tablecloths.

The diners don't dilly-dally. Apparently their time is rather strictly rationed, as in other institutions for the needy.

Only in winter do the frequenters of the place want to lengthen their stay as much as possible, in winter when a freezing wind passes through the city and those who step outside slip on sheets of filthy slush, when the skies are black and the lamplights don't penetrate the dull grayness.

They stay for the coal stove in the center of the room, for the steam. But now is the beginning of summer.

Rubi's spoon lazily stirs in the plate of soup. He's not having any apparently. His head leans on his fist.

"Eat," says the good friend. "Aren't you hungry?"

"Cold," says Rubi. "The soup's cold."

The friend smiles.

Rubi lights up an Admiral.

Then their ears catch the high blare of the trumpets, a heart-rending prelude to the marvelous victory anthem. The holy touch of dread.

"We came late this time. The soup got cold," says the friend. "We should have come here at twelve. Now it's close to two."

Rubi pushes the soup plate away. Then he extinguishes his cigarette in it and the blackened butt floats on the thick cold dough of barley and mushrooms.

"So how are you, Mordi?"

But Mordi is bewitched. The trumpets are dying out now in the distance, wonderful as they go silent. The wonder remains. He lifts his eyes and sees Rubi.

You might think that from now on a new era should begin for Rubi. After all, it's no small thing for a man to allow himself to give up a plate of soup just because it got cold. Don't the experts say that a culture is measured, among other things, by the number of its luxuries? No doubt it's a blessing and an achievement to have more than you need. The friend's sharp eyes see what's going on in Rubi's head, but grow veiled.

He himself, not long ago, entered the realm which permits the beginnings of renunciation or choice. In the middle of April he ceased licking wounds and bowing thank-yous up and down for everything they gave him. First, he restricted himself to the most important items; he attempted to put some flesh between skin and bones, to enrich a bit the sparse content of his blood.

With much effort he reached the level of the pampered who allow themselves refusal or preference. Hugger-mugger, he established for himself a sort of personal *cogito*. He said to himself, "I choose, therefore I am Mordi."

Afterward came the silence. The extended slumber interrupted by those sudden illuminations which flourish and die down. And another silence —the inauguration of the critical period. The day he allowed himself, for the first time, to renounce a portion of the menu—an act bound to join him to those who just wander—he was on his way wandering.

The seventh step, the eighth step, remained at his back like mute witnesses to some glorious victory. He wasn't an only son and didn't deserve a heap of compliments, though his accomplishment was worth some praise. Afterward he leaned against the moist, mossy wall at the bottom of the mighty stone barrackslike structure. Out of pity he permitted himself to push aside the questions that were slowly creeping upon him.

I crossed mountains of snow.

Finally he made the snap decision that he had

enough strength to leave room for others, those weaker than he on the list of unfortunates. He got up and started walking. He was sufficiently strong now not to faint. And so he did not faint. He knew where he came from, and where he was. He found it difficult to answer the implied question where to? But he traveled on. And reached this city.

After a while, Rubi also reaches this area of comprehension—as if he were one of the few to smuggle in. Mordi looks at him, at Rubi, with the particular affection typical of the handicapped or convalescent, and thinks in the remainder of his heart: "How lucky you are."

"We're closing up," says the old waiter.

"Let's go," says Mordi. The soup kitchen is empty now. The tables, an abandoned battlefield. The chairs, legs up.

"You know this city?" asks Rubi.

"More or less."

"Is Little Brothers Street far from here?"

"Why?"

"A relative of mine lives there."

"How do you know?"

"I just now remembered. My relative lives there. Attorney Salomon. You know him?"

"No."

"He's a famous lawyer. Haven't you heard of him?"

"No."

"His wife's the daughter of Dr. Hirsch. You must have heard of him?"

"No."

"That's right, you're not from here. If you were, you'd know something. Everybody knew them."

"You want to go there?"

"He's our relative. His wife's my father's sister."

"Cousins?"

"Yes. But we haven't seen each other in a long time. I hope they recognize me. Sometimes we'd travel to them, and sometimes they'd come to us. They had a daughter named Rosie and a son, Yosie. Rosie was my sister's age and Yosie was mine. Is it far from here, their street? Do you think they'll recognize me?"

"Why do you ask?"

"I want to go there."

"Don't go to them. Now, it's not worth it. Don't go."

"Why?"

"You waited, wait a bit more. Send them a short letter. Say you arrived in town and you want to visit them. Ask when its convenient for them. They'll answer you in a day or two. You'll know when to come, what day and what hour. Just like that, to knock on the door, it isn't done. Those days are over."

"But where will they send their reply? I don't

have an address, and I don't have a holding box at the post office."
"Use my address."
"You have an address?"
"Yes."
"Are you sure you have an address?"
"I have an address."
"I don't think you have an address."
"I have."
"I don't say you haven't a place to sleep, but an address is something else."
"I have, I have one."

It seems to him, it just seems to him that he has an address, says Rubi in his heart, stretched out on a bench in the imperial garden.
The Salomons will recognize me. It's a pity to waste time. He's right. He hates to waste the time that seems to be streaming away in different directions, without any purpose at all, in the manner of water breaking through dams. Such water always moves downward. He himself moves backward. A chip off the old block, like his father he keeps inside himself an old-fashioned refusal of futility and waste. So be it, the waters are a law unto themselves, and need not excuse their wasteful flow. But time belongs as much to him as to anybody. Father, without realizing it, knocked into him a

respect for time; he was always busy. Last to sleep, first to rise. He knew how to divide his life between the necessary and the worthwhile. He never wasted his time. Business and books, that was his life. And yet, amazingly enough, he always had time left over for "What did you learn today?" or a look of infinite tenderness.

One day the teacher said to Father, "Mr. Krauss, your son is a genius in mathematics."

Yes, the boy once brought up a mathematical problem that left the happy father spellbound. He took down the formulation and sent it to Professor Zultan. Professor Zultan didn't wait; he invited the student at once for a private conversation in his office, during reception hours. Father accompanied him there. The learned old man couldn't believe his eyes. A boy of thirteen stood before him. The amazed teacher rested his long, nicotined fingers on Rubi's head as if he were putting a crown on him in a ceremony. "You're lucky, Mr. Krauss," he said. Father stood silent, crushing his hat.

"Far from here?"
"Not much more."
Mordi's a good boy, he's not out to trick me. But he hasn't an address. Maybe he'll have one soon. Then the mailman will bring a letter from the

The Chocolate Deal

Salomons, and it'll say, among other things, "We're so happy. We can hardly wait. Come at once."

I'll recognize the place. There were marble steps there, if I'm not mistaken, and a red carpet. A heavy mahogany door, or a door of iron and glass. I remember: there were two doors, one to the elevator, the other to the apartment. The apartment itself took up one complete wing on the seventh floor of that magnificent, many-storied building. And the office was there, too.

Uncle Salomon didn't handle small-fry criminal cases, or minor marital disasters. He was actually a businessman, an intermediary, who drew up contracts. A lover of abstraction and imagination. Only once in a great while did he break his habit and personally handle some sort of delicate case.

Once I had a bird's-eye view of a black Mercedes skidding to a stop by the curbstone at the bottom of the tall building. A woman in black got out, on her head a straw hat strung with cherries. Uncle Salomon was waiting for her downstairs. A rare occasion. No horn sounded, no servants broke their backs bowing. Yet a sort of holiday took place. Aunt Elizabeth got rid of us.

You could hear, on the other side of the thick walls, the stifled voice of this queen and the soothing voice of Dr. Salomon.

Mainly, though, to repeat, he dealt in drawing

up contracts, in acting as advisor, mediator, representative. He kept far away from fainting women, from shattered glass, from hemorrhages, and therefore he didn't turn the defense box into a barricade, asmoke and thundering in the name of holy causes. He wasn't a famous orator and shied away from making the courthouse a theater. He preferred the light of understanding, the flash of strategy, the cunning of expediency, the powerful calmness of experience. Above all Uncle Salomon benefited from an intricate net of connections, including many whose names meant something. In a good mood he'd come out with a statement like: "I can reach every man in this country directly." Meaning every man whose name showed on his face. Then he'd pull out a jumbo cigar from its cellophane and snip one end with a utensil made for such things.

"Have a cigarette," says Mordi.
Come at once, they'll answer, we're waiting for you, Rubi, on pins and needles.
First stage: Falling on necks, and tears.
Second stage: Standing back as if before a portrait: Yes, it's Rubi!
They won't ask for further proof—hidden birthmarks, secret scars; despite everything it's Rubi.
His shoulder awaits the strong whack (Yosie);

then comes the shriek cut short by pallor and amazement (Rosie), with Aunt Elizabeth keeping up her quiet crying.

Oh, royal Uncle Salomon, how the man has grayed: Yes, yes, so he's arrived. (A modest deposit; the important speech will come later.)

And here's the maid, coming in by chance to ask something. What's her name? Mitsi or Gerti? No! The ten years that passed haven't damaged her. The opposite! Just the opposite! Now he's worthy of her. In the hot desert of a night, barefoot, crossing the endless corridors and carpets, touching the cold brass knob that turns left and opens the door (she could have locked it...). The moonlight through the drapes. August. The beach. She's very tanned, conspicuous upon the white sheet. A certain fragrance in the air, like a wandering spirit. A second sheet across her midriff like an abandoned curtain. Sunk in an eternal slumber, as if under the spell of a rare potion. Unprotected, like a city without walls. In a sweet faint. Afterward her eyes split open. But his hand is on her mouth. A tiny hint. She pulls away quietly. "Rubi, oh, Rubi."

"You're sighing," says Mordi. "We'll soon be there."

Many days later, when the night brightens, Rubi can distinguish the city's limits under the dull-gray darkness and the remarkable way the skies precisely match the surrounding hills. The city's beauty, regal but terrifically scarred, is given over now to silence. But we hear a patrol car, madly rushing down the enormous boulevards. Who will reach the dawn first? We listen. A week ago we heard a unit of soldiers pass by in boots, yellowish khaki, peaked hats, pass by singing in three part harmony. "They sing nicely," said Mordi. The street is empty now, because of the late hour and because of these soldiers with chests full of medals for heroism, rescue, death. Now they're very relaxed and stuffed with victory.

And so they are intimately familiar with birds of night. Yesterday, for instance, we surprised a bird that soared, terrified, into the dark, high regions above in order to recuperate. Rubi laughed, and Mordi thought something about birds.

Mordi has his own brand of patience. He doesn't hurry. Where should he hurry to? He has time. Occasionally Rubi reads frightful ideas in his face. When they go beyond what's permissible, when Mordi looks lost in a long dream, Rubi cries out, "Mordi!" And, like a man waking up, he returns from his distances, only to smile.

"What are you thinking about?"
"Nothing. Really nothing."
"Mordi, what are you thinking about?"
"I told you, nothing. Nothing, really, nothing."

The Chocolate Deal

Sometimes the two separate for a while, so as to meet once again. Rubi goes to get food and clothes. It's the beginning of fall. Mordi waits for him, and waits for him, in order to take him along to his house, his address.

Rubi has to meet his Salomons, and I prevent him. Another day, that's nothing, another two days. No reason to hurry, there's plenty of time. Even if we use up a considerable portion of it, more than enough would remain for us, enough and more.

We'll do the same things all over again. We'll walk many days. We'll sit whole hours. We'll ask: Whom, for instance, could we expect to meet just like that, suddenly, the way we two met? What's certain? Maybe we'll go from here to another land, we'll go and try it out. Meanwhile we can look for an address. It's not easy, I know. Many houses are shut and covered with soot, and others are too blown open. But in the meantime we have to move and think and change. We'll go and adjust ourselves accordingly. Perhaps we'll succeed, and then we'll be so different and far away we can make a new start in a new place. We'll get other clothes. Get other names. Where's Rubi hurrying to? Why does he hurry so much? He runs. Me, I don't run, even though we have to find a substitute for this city park. It's still summer now, but soon

... Yes. Something must be done. But I don't want to do more than this. We'll find something. And then? He always asks me: And then what? Everything widens so much. Becomes so uncrowded. And there's plenty of extra room. And various possibilities.

The Salomons, Rubi again recites to himself. The gate to salvation. Oh, this will be a reunion to end all reunions. Afterward, through Uncle Salomon's connections, I'll be helped. Why not? For a relative. The family. A short cut. The ascent. Gerti. Since he renounced the soup, many days have passed. That time is dead. Harvesting is over; summer gone. A woman, his good advisers told him; she's an unavoidable stage on the way. Not to mention those terrible awakenings on the bench, the pictures he created in his dream. Cigarette in his fist. Heavy head reddening on his right hand that goes paler and paler. Confusion: his cart's before his horse.

"What are you thinking about, Rubi?"

"Nothing, really, nothing."

One day he said, "Mordi, you know, it's been a long time since I touched a woman."

We walk and walk, and get nowhere, thinks Rubi, his suspicion mounting, and here it's already the rainy season. Leaves are falling. It's chilly. I'm in summer clothes. The police don't like us. And soon neither will the weather. Only the statues feel good at night.

"We're here," says Mordi.
"It's hard to call this an address." Rubi smiles. "I think it's an abandoned warehouse, pretty bad. A single person content with almost nothing could barely make do here."
"It's not permanent lodgings."
"Who gave you this room?"
"I inherited it."
"Who gave you this room?"
The skies are stiff as lead; a bad, cold rain.
"Come inside," says Mordi. "Come, we'll work it out somehow. There are more than forty centimeters for each of us. Meantime write the letter to your uncle."
"You're right," says Rubi. "Actually, it's orderly enough here; clean."
"In school I got excellent for order and cleanliness, remember?"
"Do you have stationery?"
"I think I have something in my suitcase; wait a minute."
"Thanks, Mordi, thanks a lot."
Outside the flood begins.

Dear Uncle Salomon:

Do you remember me, Reuben Krauss, Rubi, the son of Rachel and David, Hannah's brother? I've been in this city for about half a year, lodging in the flat of my good friend from gymnasium days, Mr. Mordecai Neuberg. I'd be very happy if you'd let me know, in your reply, when I could come to your house and see your dear faces. Kindly please give, in my name, the best of my blessings to dear Aunt Elizabeth and also dear Yosie and Rosie.

With deep respect and love,
Yours, *Reuben Krauss*

My address: Reuben Krauss, c/o Neuberg, Convent of The Merciful Sisters, 2 Friedrich Street.

"When do you think the answer will arrive?"

"It depends."

Perhaps they already came back from the beaches, from the spas, from the south. They always used to return toward autumn. They and Gerti. Then the city would be filled with those worthy of it, after being in the hands of the poor during those long, desolate, furnace-hot days.

Here they come, from the lakes and woods and beaches, from the international hotels, from pine groves and marble palaces and palm trees, from feasts on the wide balcony under linen umbrellas. Girls and vigor at the Casino beach. Girls of sun and water.

The terrible hours of afternoon. Only the motionless remains outside, handed over to the mercy of the sun. And life hides itself in the shade, behind stone walls, in the now-hot now-cool shade which throws off the dying, fainting fragrance of roses and geraniums: There, there, long ago though, he saw Gerti undress absent-mindedly, giving him a supply of charms for a long journey. The poison of longings.

Southern vacation cities. Hazy. Florentine walls. Marble. Fountains.

But for now, autumn rain. The city, dark-gray, water color. They should be here, as always, with the start of the new school year, with the opening of the new season of plays, exhibitions, concerts. Less and less of the short day remains, the sun is setting early. The capital city is purple, and obscure. And already it's night.

"What do you mean: 'It depends'?"

"It depends."

But time is passing and I don't have any time; my time's over, and what'll happen if nothing happens? This is madness. What have I done? There's no remedy for squandered liquid gold. All the stolen goods of the past won't be returned nor will the thefts of the present. And nobody sees the loan. And the interest keeps rising. I'm left behind, further back than behind. Again and again they defeat me there. It's already raining now. October. Look, they've removed one defect from the ruined church. They've started raising the bridge, scraping away the moss from the iron. Fixing the stone lions so they can still gape, as in the past, throats open for ever and ever. Along the row of horsemen, the power lines are repaired. The left hand of Jesus, with its stream of blood, is carefully nailed to the cross for the second time. The shop windows remember to shut off their lights, and soon winter shall come. Nobody will stop it. The marble and bronze horses shall continue to bear kings and sword-drawn battle commanders on their backs who direct their penetrating glances into the gathering clouds and snow. Middle-aged men, thick-eyebrowed, tight-jawed. And atop the War Ministry Building shall soar the proud, ancient, iron eagles.

Afterward spring will come like a despised solution, nothing uglier than itself. That foul downpour shall begin, endlessly collecting in wadis and ravines and still lower, into rivers and the never-filled sea. Then spring shall be given permission to turn the wild forests green, like a numbness returning with its own murderous dullness.

"What's the meaning of 'It depends'?"

"A day more. A day less. A matter of two or three days."

"I could have gone to them at once. You're a good boy, Mordi, but it's not clear to me why I waited and waited."

But Mordi doesn't answer.

"I could have waited by their house. Just waited. Gerti would pass. I'd place myself right in front of her. She'd finally recognize me; she might scream or fall down, but in the end she'd recognize me."

"That's not the way it's done," says Mordi.

"Why not?"

"It's not done."

Rubi: "Gerti, tell Uncle Salomon I'm here. Waiting. Downstairs."

Uncle Salomon: "Why are you quiet there? Bring him in! Bring him in at once!" And echo upon echo flies through the never-ending apartment, breaking against the corridors: "Elizabeth! Elizabeth! Yosie! Rosie! He's here!"

"Why isn't it done?"

"I'm just advising you."

"You're just advising me."

"What have I done to you, Rubi, why are you mad at me? Why do you hate me?"

"Mordi, don't talk like a fool! Me, angry at you? Me?"

Because you're burying me here beside you, in this grave. And me, I have no time, I have relatives waiting for me on pins and needles. Day and night. Uncle Salomon says: "Maybe Rubi will come. He was a talented, strong boy. Of course he'll come. Where were you? Elizabeth, Gerti, get some food ready, prepare something for him!" And Gerti replies: "I'd rather he washed up first. A hot bath. In the meantime I'll prepare him something."

Without doubt, a chain of simultaneous activities is somewhat marvelous; you're washing yourself and at the same time the coffee warms up for you and at the same time the telephone rings: "Hello, Alfred, guess who's here with us! No . . . no . . . I'll tell you. Should I?" And Gerti, busy by the stove. He was a young boy. And now, a man. A trembling man. A man in her presence.

"I'm not angry at you, but there's no use waiting. It's a pity to waste time."

"You're right."

"You see?"

Then Sister Theresa enters, carrying bread and coffee.

"Thank you, Sister Theresa, never shall we forget you for this," says Mordi.

"It's nothing, it's nothing," says the excited Sister. "You gentlemen must be hungry."

"Never shall we forget her for this," laughs Rubi. "Never."

And another possibility, the possibility of that terrible fire.

What exactly do you mean? What fire are you talking about?

About the frightful fire which often breaks out. Here or some other place, in a building so engulfed by flames that all its windows are mouths of gold, of purple, of thick black smoke. Sodom and Gomorrah.

Ah, then the spectators circle around and freeze, to see what's going on. Someone says twice, as if to himself, "Something must be done!" Because in the meantime the building is left burning. Others cross themselves. A building of many stories, magnificent, crowded. Then the siren of the fire trucks is heard approaching, that terrifying rushing wail, reminder of salvation that has often come too late. The dramas enacted there recall the very first catastrophe, Primordial Chaos. The trucks don't wait another second and attack the fire with giant hoses. At first it looks as if, in haste, they've used oil instead of water for with the power of a furnace, lo, the flames rise, forcing all human life to flee far away, faces charred and choking from the smoke. And there above, the porches crowded with those despairing. Ah, who created, in his cockeyed dream, a vision so absurd, so gorgeous? For what purpose? What frenzied poet turned his sick imagination or his blind desire for revenge into fact? What does he, Rubi, have to do with all this? Why did the fire seize this respectable apartment house, and who's the arsonist? What crooked, rotten logic ties together by flames, in a Hell of a celebration after the pattern of burning Rome, household objects, books, pianos, original paintings? Who can talk about paintings now? Who has a head for paintings? Now, as the fire mounts higher and higher despite the rescue efforts of more and more firemen summoned here from distant quarters.

"Children!" shouts someone. "There are children over there!"

And while in some windows water gains the upper hand, forcing the fire to submit to a black extinction of stinking smoke and wet ashes, at others the flames still climb, celebrate.

At that moment the lodgers who are daring and light on their feet leap into the tarpaulin nets stretched out underneath them like giant squares.

"Jump!" they shout from below, on loudspeakers. And the daring leap. By ones and twos.

But what will the blond-haired little girl do? In this so unexpected development, what will she do, at her age?

"Jump!" begs the crowd. "Jump!" Women pull out their hair, and those who can't stand the sight faint or flee.

"Jump!" gasp the smoke-choked firemen, blackened and half-scorched.

"Give me a wet blanket and a ladder," says Rubi.

"A wet blanket!" Voices go up on all sides. "A ladder! A ladder! Get him a ladder! Get him a ladder! Get him a blanket! Get him a wet one!"

At once they bring him a heavy, water-soaked woolen blanket, and set up a ladder. He wraps himself and starts climbing with a firm grip and the quickness of a cat, rung after rung, up and up, till he's lost in a dark cloud. As if on the merit of Mishael and Azariah.

And the moment is one of paralyzed astonishment. It looks as if the firemen, too, are dropping their equipment in order not to miss these few seconds, to see how he reaches the seventh floor, the top floor, a burning angel groping in the thick smoke, how he embraces the helpless child, wraps her in the blanket, and sinks down from the heights with her, down and down, a long while, into the taut firemen's net that appears from above like a handkerchief.

They open the blanket. Separate the entwined couple. The child stretches out a hand to the fire chief who lifts and carries her aside. Then the weeping begins. Many just stand and weep. The fire goes out like a quietening animal.

Reporters come and circle him, Rubi, with questions. They bend over and take his picture or rise on their toes, extending their arms way up, and snap their cameras.

A man of about fifty stands there. "Let him through! Let him through!"

"I'm her father," says the man. "I came just this minute. I saw everything."

They photograph the father. Hand him his daughter and photograph the two of them.

"How can I thank you? How can I repay you?"

"I did my duty," says he, Rubi, and breaks the hearts of those gathered around. Truly, there's nothing, not even salt in the eyes, that arouses so much genuine feeling as the sight of heroism, that self-sacrifice, body and soul, which the heroes themselves consider a matter of course—those heroes who clam up before thank-yous and hurrahs.

Dr. Hoffman was a successful skin doctor.

The Chocolate Deal

The papers are black with giant headlines and pictures:

"GIRL OF TEN RESCUED FROM BURNING HOUSE. A RARE DISPLAY OF COURAGE."

"Reuben (Rubi) Krauss, a refugee without citizenship status and without work, who lives with his friend in a little cellar in the courtyard of The Merciful Sisters Convent, yesterday displayed an unusual daring by climbing a fireman's ladder up to the seventh floor of a burning house and rescuing the only daughter of Dr. Karl Hoffman. The man embraced the girl and leaped with her into the rescue net held by the firemen. The girl emerged from the accident only slightly shaken up."

"Charlotte Hoffman is in perfect condition."

"The City Hospital has informed us that the medical examination has found Charlotte Hoffman in perfect condition."

Other papers deemed it necessary to rebuke the firemen for leaving the act of rescue to an unknown who happened to pass by. "What will happen next time?" asks *Express*. "Who will save our children?" And they clamor about "criminal neglect in the alarm system and in the quality of the fire equipment."

Uncle Salomon will read about it. Will hear it on the radio. Will see my picture. Will yell: "Hey, it's Rubi! It's our Rubi! Elizabeth! Elizabeth!"

That's starting on the right foot. I'll be able to sell the story of my life, because they're bound to ask me questions. Who am I, and what am I? Where do I come from? Where am I staying? And where am I heading?

"Rubi, don't start up."
"I won't start up. I won't start up."
"I'm not to blame."
"I didn't say anything."
"What did the Sisters do to you?"
"The dear Sisters."
"They don't deserve to be mocked. They're so good, so different, so remote."
"They fulfill their duty."
"What duty?"
"Their duty from the division of duties."
"What division of duties?"
"Others kill, and they have mercy. The day will come when these pale, sad women in black shall rage, attack, slaughter. Then the murderers will hasten to our aid, comfort us, serve us a glass of water and, by our blood-stained beds, cross themselves in silence. For the sake of change. Oh, then will salvation come . . ."

"Have a cigarette, Rubi."

"Thanks. I was only joking."

"They're so kind, so quiet. What would we do without them?"

"What are you doing?"

"Nothing. Pipe-dreaming wonders."

"I understand. Soon you'll be way up there, on top."

"What'll I do there?"

"You'll be a genius. You'll verify Professor Zultan's theories, to the joy of your parents' and teachers' hearts—you favorite son."

"Meanwhile I have to find a woman."

"And afterward you'll be a great mathematician."

"Meanwhile I have to find a woman."

"Right."

"If we lived in a cellar with a houseful of sewing girls above, or bank girls, or girl students, we'd have a good life. We'd keep going up and up."

"Going where?"

"Up, by the power of their dreams. Go know what these nuns dream at night. Most likely they always dream they're being loved."

"That's enough."

"In their dreams they're always being loved

hard, with unbelievable coarseness and no words, and they get pregnant."

"Quit it, Rubi."

"And then they get up to pray, to chase the evil spirits away through silent prayer. They glance at the image near their beds of the suffering one and slowly calm down so as to purify themselves, in heart-rending stillness, on beds of poverty and loneliness."

"What did you say?"

"I didn't say a thing."

"I thought you said something about the nuns."

"I didn't speak."

"Excuse me."

"Oi, Mordi, Mordi, what'll be the end of you?"

"He'll leave soon. In order to be among the called. He'll find happiness. Yes, he'll be among the called. They'll discover him and want him. Very nice. And what next?"

"He'll start to wander."

"He'll wander and wander and become a different person, far far away. Our hosts will have to cut fifty per cent of their dole of mercy and compassion. He'll meet women wearing colored dresses. You'll remain all alone, Mordi. Why aren't you dead?"

"Because they didn't see me."

"If only Moshko were in your place."

"You're right."

"Too bad about Moshko. What a great fellow. Life needs men like him. They beautify the world. They give it strength and laughter."

"Where is he now?"

"Up high, my friend, up high, contributing disquiet and longing to heaven."

"They hanged him."

"I didn't know."

"I know you didn't. You liked him a lot. You were good friends."

"He was a terrible student but a good fellow."

"You want to say that the sweet mercy of the miracle was wasted on me. It was a bad mistake."

"Quit it."

"Yes. You want to say I don't deserve the favor that came my way."

"I didn't say that."

"If only Moshko were in my place..."

"Quit it, Mordi, quit it. That hurts."

"Moshko used to give back all the thefts, all of them."

"I didn't say that."

"Moshko used to take Hannah."

"What Hannah?"

"Hannah, Hannah."

"Leave Hannah out of it. What do you want from her?"

"She didn't tell you?"
"Tell me what?"
"I thought she told you."
"About you?"
"About me or about him."
"Hannah."
"I just asked."
"Huh."
"Too bad about him."
"Don't start up."
"You said it."
"What did I say?"
"If only Moshko were . . ."
"I was joking."
"Joking?"
"Joking. I swear it."
"Of course you were joking."
"Believe me, just joking."
"Yes, you were just joking."
"You're funny, Mordi. You're funny."
"Kidding aside, I'm beside Hannah there, and Moshko's here with you. If he were, what would he do?"
"Oh, Moshko would do very nicely. He couldn't live any other way. Today he'd be a rich man."
"You think . . ."
"I guess he'd be rich."
"Interesting."

The Chocolate Deal

"His type start from nothing and get rich as porters or rag-dealers. When unemployment hits the rag-dealers, they pour out their urine on grinding stones for a small fee, or they whet their tongues in post offices to help paste on the stamps, or they straighten bananas, or sell charms for the birth of sons. Afterward they disappear, for a short or a long while, and reappear on the list of oil magnates or tin magnates or newspaper magnates or gold or water magnates."

"What are you talking about?"

"Men like him don't go to waste."

"Moshko, my dead king."

"Stop crying."

"What a loss!"

"Stop crying, I say. Stop crying. If you won't stop, I'm not responsible for what I do. If you keep up that crying, I don't know what will happen here. No, no, really, Mordi, stop crying, you hear me, don't cry, do me a favor. Enough. I didn't say a thing. That's all. Enough. That's enough. I mean it. You want a cigarette? Take a cigarette. Take one. Take a cigarette. Come, let's go outside. Let's walk around a bit. Go some place. Do something. It's already late. It won't arrive today. Not the letter and not Dr. Hoffman's check. Tomorrow's another day. Come."

"Where will we go?"

"We'll just go. What do you care? We'll go. The main thing is going. I don't want to stay here. Come, come. If you're my friend, come. Come, come!"

"I won't go with you."

"Why, for what reason, why?"

"Because I'm not Moshko."

"That's not important. Forget Moshko. Moshko doesn't exist. That's all there is to it. Period."

"You don't need me."

"You're talking nonsense."

"Why should you?"

"Why should I what?"

"Why should you need me? I'd be a burden to you."

"Cut it out!"

"Should I tell you who I am?"

"Don't tell me who you are. No thanks. I know what you'll tell me. 'I am the disease, Rubi, the disease that accompanies you. I am the pallor that drops upon you when you require fresh strength. I am the cough that attacks you. Your red eyes. I'm the question marks . . .' You make me laugh, Mordi; you want me to plead before you, to repeat that you're a good fellow, a bit too sensitive, that you look into things too much. I came to a city where nobody knew me, but nobody. I met you. We walked together. Ate together. You spread out wide summer palaces before me: the imperial garden and the statue garden and the zoo. And in winter you gave me your address, this room. A roof between me and the rain. And soon the first snow will fall. You want me to thank you all over again from the bottom of my heart. I thank you all over again. All that you did for me, I know, couldn't be taken for granted. You were the first to meet me, and I'll be the last to forget that. Are you satisfied now. Yes?"

"Stop it, Rubi, don't thank me. Go ahead. Take a walk. Go see a movie. Go find a woman."

"Come with me."

"Next time. I'll try it myself. Next time. Not now. Go. Go ahead. I'll wait for you. What's the difference to you? Go alone. I'll stay here; finish a few unfinished letters."

"You'll stay here and be good, very good. I don't want that. Come along!"

The silence stretches.

"No, Rubi," he says as I figured he would, "I swear it's not a fair division of duties."

Apparently he continues: "What in the world do you need me for?! A ball and chain? A yoke? It's amazing how light you'd be without me. You'd get what's coming to you through merit and not mercy. Beware of me, you're liable to make a bad bargain. I'm liable to ruin you."

"Stop, don't talk nonsense."

"I'm liable to turn you into a total wanderer in a world of chaos, a world where even the song of a bird will seem sin's accomplice to you, where the rains of spring . . ."

"I have nothing against rain, and birds."

". . . where the rains of spring take part in fading footprints, where the grass has covenanted with bastards and the rainbow is a terrible joke in skies of sun and rain. Mockery."

"You're dreaming, Mordi. Mordi, sit; sit down a minute. Where are you going?"

". . . where each of your walks is considered a wicked choice."

"Why, Mordi? What have I done to you?"

"That's why I said go. I can't propose a thing."

"What do you want from me?"

"Nothing. I swear it! Go, Rubi. Go to a movie, or go to a woman. You haven't done that in a long time. You need it. I read it in your eyes. Not far off, by the market, there's a cheap, clean place."

"Were you there?"

"I wasn't, but I know."

"How?"

"I've walked around in that area."

"And you'll wait for me here."

"Yes."

"What do you advise me to do?"

"Why ask me?"

"You're a smart man and I need your advice."
"I told you."
"You were about to tell me."
"Go. Get out of here. Time's passing. It's a shame."
"Nonsense."
"Why nonsense?"
"Because you don't ask me."
"I'm asking."

Am I really asking? I didn't turn to him for advice before climbing that fireman's ladder. Right. He wasn't at my side. And I didn't have time. In such cases, the important thing is speed. If I hadn't acted at once, the business would've been lost. When did I climb? Who climbed?

For a long while we converse by means of such unspoken guesses, as in a prison.

"But he's mad at me. He's not mad."
"Is he sad?"
"Yes."
"Why?"
"Not right now."
"Okay."
"In order to go back to the good old days, to the chivalry, the compassion, and the magnanimity."

In his head, Rubi assigns thoughts to his dear friend and explains to him with a certain formality: "I hate the combination, girl and fire; and besides, I want to do something. I don't want them to keep on taking care of me. I don't want to keep searching for my name on the list of the missing. I want to jump from here into another place. Always moving. To show them. I'll go on living. You see? I'm not dead. They haven't confiscated my name. And I haven't forgotten the names of the others. When they managed to bend me, I wasn't in the family of boot-lickers, and when my own teeth devoured my flesh, I wasn't in the family of rats, and when they actually deceived me, I wasn't in the family of fools, I was just a man who had been taken in."

"Why are you telling me all this?" he'll ask.

"Because I have no shame," I'll answer.

"That's too miserable a cure. Most of the defeated use it after a while. You'll see. A worthless excuse. To give you the right to raise your head. Isn't that so, Rubi?" he'll ask.

"Mordi, you often fall asleep for hours. For days. Yesterday you fell asleep sitting up. I went out to look for Gerti. I passed by the Opera House. And I saw a picture: Four American soldiers in a jeep stopped alongside a crowd of people lined up for *Tosca*. One of them, intoxicated apparently, yelled, 'I'm a good boy, I'm a good boy!' and threw a fistful of coins into the crowd, and did it again, as if he were sowing. The crowd, frozen stiff before, waked from its deep sleep. A hand-to-hand battle began, with howls and shrieks. And while the sea roared, the young soldiers laughed. Gerti wasn't there."

Where are you, Gerti? In a night like this I need you. Very much. It's hard without you. I look for you and look for you. It's impossible for you not to sense it, for you to go on sleeping as if nothing has happened, as if you hadn't lain awake on your back a whole night through, and yet another night, expecting the door to squeak and announce me, when it was altogether hopeless, when you said and said again: He never ever existed. As if I hadn't come to you then, always the next to last minute, and you almost fainting at my coming to give you yourself again. I remember all this. It's impossible that on such a night, for instance, you won't howl from pain and from loneliness because I'm not inside you once more, like the inevitable, the desired unto tears, a slow sacred ceremony with each part inseparable from the deep ecstasy of your magnificent body. Am I right? I keep far far behind me the illusions of your fantasy, and I turn your hopes into things past, I eliminate all your yearnings, fill you with vast measures of joy. No! It's impossible for you not to come out incessantly to meet me now. Lost and stumbling. Where is he? If he doesn't come right away, you'll lose the last of your mind, because you can't go on without me, because you're used to me, to the special poetry that accompanies my long journeys inside you, a poetry matched by the phantasmagoria hovering over your closed eyes. "Enough?" I'd ask. "Enough?" And you'd have no strength for an answer. Then you asked one of your waning smiles to represent you; then you slept on your shoulder, a woman after.

Where are you now, where are you? I sent a letter to Uncle Salomon and await an answer any minute. Actually I could have taken a short cut and gone right to his house, knocked on the door, but I refrained from doing so on account of the advice of my friend, Mordi Neuberg, whom you don't know. A good boy, sensitive, but very broken up because he advised me to wait for a reply. Meanwhile summer went by. You traveled south, to the sea, to the palms, as always. The apartment is locked with iron bolts. At last he took me along to his room in a cellar. Meantime, as you know, I became famous in the newspapers and on the radio. You've seen the picture taken of me for my feat of rescue a few weeks ago: I climbed a fireman's ladder to the seventh floor of a burning building and snatched down a girl, the only daughter, they tell me, of a famous skin doctor, Karl Hoffman. I received thank-yous and praise and secretly I'm still

The Chocolate Deal

hoping for some sort of check. By the way, I want to take this opportunity to tell you that I've decided to become rich. Nothing to wonder at. I was destined for it. I'm the essence of talent and initiative and imagination. They've restrained me, as you know, but I keep moving. You see, I walk in snow, and on and on I walk. It's possible to rob men of their talents without robbing their lives. My talents are back, they greet me. I need you as a private secretary, as a mistress. We'll go far. You'll see just how far we'll go.

RUBI WENT FOR A WALK, something to do. He must have found a woman. To take my place. Right to the point, finally. What can I give him, what? And she, him? And he, her? Depending on the shoulders. Depending on the chin. She'll pay him in the end. He deserves it. I'm sick. A gray-beard one thousand and thirty years old. I tried to take in. Here and there. And it's hard for me. I'm so taken in. On all sides. My body's not sound. He, at least, has the arms for grabbing. The stubborn hold. The cheek of the unrestrained. See, he gets up on his feet and goes and goes and goes. And now I measure the distance growing between us. Fortune or fate? What wouldn't I give to have the chance, the prospect, once in a while, of being someone. Samson for one night. I'd give all I have. That's not much. As a bonus I'd pledge my last belongings and personal talents and the honor of a doctor's degree. Were Moshko alive, at least. It'd be easier for me, without any doubt. And I have nothing to sell and nothing to buy. They know me.

The Chocolate Deal

It's written on my face as it was then, for example, in that very house, on that very street; Joy Street they call it, that's what the sign says, black on white. It branches off to the right of Big Field Street.

I stood there, I remember, for hours. Finally it was nine or nine-thirty. My heart full of ice.

A one-story house, flat, with opaque windows, but its door wide open so you could look in.

There was a reception room, long and smoke-filled, and a pianist who played like a madman, paining the piano, to get the most out of a shocking folk song. There were men who came and women waiting for them, and tables, and bottles, and hot dogs and pepper. I was there. The men came and went, and the women remained there, waiting. No. Not frozen in expectation. No. After fantastic amounts of brandy, they laughed as if they were at some big once-in-a-life-time celebration. Dressed in flowered house robes. The place was too large for a reception room or a bar, and the corridors splitting off from it led to many rooms.

The pianist kept playing. Kept playing light melodies. Those who knew what they wanted took some of the waiting women and disappeared with them. While other women moved over to the hesitant, pushing up close against them, tracing a titillating journey on their chests with a long finger, and making them laugh. They drew them on and on.

As soon as the first-comers left, others took their places and began to smoke or just disappear or put their faces to a wall, stock-still, and additional men came and saw the additional women and felt them all over as though they were goods for sale, and whispered into their ears a joke that made them nearly collapse from laughter, and they had a ball, and in return the additional women got hold of them and drew them on, and brought them to the little rooms, to the filthy beds.

But I stood there and they didn't pull me along and I didn't draw them on or introduce myself. Finally they saw me and said, "Sir, what are you doing here?"

I said, "I came here like all the rest. What's the matter?"

They said, "It's late. We're closing up now. Come another time."

The pianist shut the piano, got up, kissed the hand of an old tired woman. And left.

Why am I forbidden to be there? And how do they know who I am? It's written on my forehead: Come to see, to try. What fears! For me it should have been different; one by one, in a roundabout manner, they should have come to me and trusted me. I haven't yet had a taste of it, but I'm strong enough. I just need the opportunity, the right moment. Wait a moment, something's still not clear to me here, it must be cleared up in order to shorten my route, make it a straight line. And that's that. How Moshko behaved over the sculpture business at Nador's, when the four of us went there, Rubi and Hannah and Moshko and me. By the way, where's Nador now? What's left of his garret, his studio?

He lived there. Closed off. By himself. A graying bachelor, a powerful man, forever sloppy, in filthy corduroy pants and a red flannel shirt. His long hands were amazingly handsome, most likely because of that rare combination of strength and sensitivity. But he didn't know this. And so he was unique. He had no time to peek into the mirror, to see his forest of a chest, his narrow face, patterned, unconsciously, after one of the forms that filled the room—mortification and desire.

We used to go there a lot. Sometimes we found his students there laboring at his side like apprentices. He worked in various materials—gypsum, stone, wood, and iron. Once in a while this or that girl would come, to be silent beside him, or prepare him some coffee, or stay over till the next day. They say he was married once, that he had a son from that marriage.

He attempted to find the soul of his materials

and that soul's embodiment in the different forms he sought to shape in its image, without much self-satisfaction, haunted always by the poisoning suspicion that he was slipping into the unnecessary and bewilderment. The studio was full of beginnings, lumps half-finished like interrupted sentences, advance payments for the days of grace, days of serenity and strength. When he was tired he'd dabble in jewelry-making or experiment with decorations. That's what he called those paintings made from sheets of glass, with all kinds of materials from daily life inserted—paper and colored cloth, or tin, or net.

In this room he lived and ate his meals. Empty bottles of wine and crusts of bread, tin cans and left-over yellowed cheese, testified to that.

Hannah admired him and she dragged us there, upstairs, like a pilgrim going up to a temple. And we three followed her footsteps.

The evening we last came to see him, he got up from his tumbled bed, glad to greet us. But then he lay down to rest, finally happy and at peace to see his work approaching his image of it after a day-long struggle with his materials.

Hannah paled. Poor thing. In such situations her blood always rushed from her face. We sat on his footstools, surrounded by the equipment and scrap material and cigarette butts of his workshop.

Pointing the way to a final wooden head were

three other wooden heads, more or less the same, that seemed to him, for some reason, failures. They were bent in disgrace and quiet on the scarred, splintered, wide worktable.
"What'll you do with these?" asked Moshko.
"I don't know."
"Let me have one."
"Which?"
"The third, that one by the wall."
"Take it."
Moshko wrapped it in cloth. We sipped coffee. We chattered. Nador hinted he'd soon be leaving to roam around a bit, to get away and see things. His room was filled with yearnings: "I have no money. But we'll see."
When we left him and descended the endless number of steps, it was evening out. Hannah, silent. "He's a charming man, isn't he?" said Moshko. Then she started to cry. Why and what for she would not say. Afterward I realized what it was all about. She had always dreamed of possessing a sculpture of his and hadn't known how to ask. Hadn't dared.
Just like me. Roundabout. Someone else comes over and takes. It doesn't matter now. A tiny paltry injustice, a meaningless toy. Now all things are level, straightened and flattened out. Here and there some structures sprout way up, like land-

marks memorializing one thing or another. Good; so what? Four heads, one of which finally seemed to him to come close to being acceptable. Moshko took one. Two were ostracized. Who took them? Who, finally, took away Nador and Hannah and Moshko, with his wooden head? And what will happen to the unfinished sculptures there, to the advance payments, to the question tied up with the tormenting of these materials into shape? What about the fears of the man? How not to lie? And how to eternalize the unique.

These questions disturbed Nador. So he wasn't different from the other artists. But he was, I remember, crueler than many. And terrifically patient. Hannah knew this. What broke her up, then, walking alongside us that evening in the street? That the business ended so quickly? Nador's careless generosity? Moshko's foolish but lovely lightheadedness? Her painful shyness? Her roundabout, devious ways? The time she needed to put together the words of her request? On the edge of fatigue she must have summed up like this: "Nador, if I were rich, I'd buy this head. I'm very fond of it. It has poetry and mystery."

What are you doing here? You're not from here? Go back to your Hannah. Look, they're preparing to marry her off to me now. Thank you. I'm going to take her unto me, return to the city where I was born, and meet nothing. As if I suddenly deserved, in exchange for her, the blue voids.

After all, I went west to study, west to write up my doctoral work on troubadour poetry. Before the flood. Afterward things happened, and I didn't grasp them. One day my professor said: "It's hard to imagine you'll be able to finish your work under these conditions. Come with me, I'll take you in my car to my brother Phillip. He lives in a little monastery not far from here, a matter of an hour-and-a-half's driving. He'll hide you. When everything's over, you'll return to me and once again we'll discuss things. We'll be able to publish your book. You've done admirable work. A contribution to the subject."

He drove fast and chose forgotten roads.

"I don't know what's happening. I don't understand a thing," he said to me, "but you'd better hide. They're looking everywhere. There are big cellars there, wine cellars. Perhaps the time will pass more quickly than we expect and we'll meet again. Let's hope there'll be a point to talking. Everything's too strange now. Just as there are earthquakes, so there are, among men, timequakes."

He spoke about fierce quakes of time that fix the boundaries of ages, about the eclipse of all light, about the disappearance of Providence. "My brother Phillip will take care of you. He knows everything."

The iron gate opened at last. The three of us stood there, the brother in a black frock. "I'm putting my best student in your hands," he told his brother, who squeezed my hand tightly without saying a word.

I became a man of darkness. They hid me in the most secret and forgotten chamber of the cellar. They gave me food and drink. A lamp, paper, and a pencil.

I had a few books.

Alone in a silence cold from dampness, amid the sour fragrance of wine silently fermenting, wine that, in the gloom, turns the ripeness of the sun-drenched vintage grapes into a bold strength, into joy, into gates that open, into the ancient melodies of suffering love. Dreaming. An eternal prisoner am I, in cells of loneliness and endless time. Unbounded, the last, day-dreaming. I'm not allowed to get up suddenly and ask: "Wait a minute, wait a minute, what is going on here? And what am I doing here?" To ascend, to climb the winding stone steps smoothed by all the tracking up and down, climbing high before the awful blindness of waking.

The Chocolate *Deal*

One long dream. Over and over I tell myself the truth so as not to totter, so as not to fall silent, down and out. Altogether ignorant. I don't get any newspapers. Good Phillip, the loyal brother, comes down from time to time and sits with me, refusing to discuss events with me. He avoids risks. He comes, it seems, to assure me that everything's all right, and that I was fated to spend the time this way and finally emerge. He prays for me too. That's no small matter.

Sometimes, at night, he pulls me upstairs for a walk, to air me out. I see the big building, its windows lit here and there. I breathe the champagne air, the pines that continue to exude their resin as if they didn't belong here. We wander together underneath many stars. He gives me the main points about what's going on. Orients me. Enlightens me a bit. But he doesn't know a thing about his brother. One report says . . . It's the time for far-off reports and birds to carry the news.

Then, without a stop, fall the winter rains. If he could only let me go upstairs to greet winter. But there are patrols. There's the chitchat of passers-by, and the near-breaking-point pressure of the secret. And I can't rely on miracles. As if I were more important than I am. In the last analysis, who am I? And how does that old shingled house fit into the map of fields, ravines, orchards, burnt brick walls? That's how it is. They brought me a stove so I wouldn't freeze in the cold coming down from the north.

A room two by two-and-a-half. An iron bed, 190 by 80 by 50 centimeters. A lamb's-wool mattress jailed in a checkered gray-blue-brown and again gray-blue-brown cloth, forty stripes and a half-stripe. And a wooden table with a drawer in it. An old-fashioned piece of furniture, scarred with inscriptions, lines, candle wax, and a burn from a forgotten cigarette. That's where my lamp is. During the day, in summer, a faint slip of light filters through the tiny, arched and barred window, casting shadows and silence into the room. In winter my lamp burns nonstop.

Sometimes I climb onto the table, peek out the window over the thick wall and see 30 by 30 centimeters of world. And hear voices.

I return to this grave. Host to a company of coarse, cold, sad stones, knowing them by heart to the last dent. I follow with my eyes the complete length of the wooden table along its grains, then move on to the grains of the chair, to the two dark-brown knots in its left leg.

Sometimes I get a fly who isn't afraid of me as a visitor.

The Chocolate Deal

My beard doesn't stop growing. "I'll bring you a scissors," says Phillip. He does all that's necessary, yet he won't talk with me about myself and my hiding. That way he spares the two of us any extra grief. He knows more than I do.

Yes, from time to time a bird comes to his window and settles there, bringing him the requested news. Then, to recuperate for a minute or two, it flies to a powerful old tree that rises up beside a wall of mossy time-heavy stone.

Yes, I read it on his face. He doesn't tell me all he knows. He asks me how my literary work is coming. No, he's not dull, I'm sure of that. He's guided by a correct, cautious feeling. He's a closed person and pensive and silent most of the time. I too have learned to keep silent.

One night I wanted to get up and go, go east, to my home town. What am I doing here in this cellar cell, by big wine barrels, in these alien depths? Hiding. Hiding because they're searching for me without letup. Why do they need someone like me? Laughter has now taken the place of pride in me. I'm beginning to look like a quiet lunatic.

Then I thought that periodically I'd shriek one day-long shriek which would earn me the title of Champion Shrieker. Maybe I was afraid of the echo that might double and triple in strength and ricochet throughout these cellars. I'd accomplish nothing that way. If my shriek were able to help me, I wouldn't need it. See, actually my lengthy silence acquires for me a unique tranquillity. Yes, tranquillity is my beloved, or something very similar. There's a logic to things. Look, you've covered half the way, or look, days are now coming, etc.

One night I started shrieking this shriek until blood filled my eyes, until sand filled my throat: Why here? And how long, just how long? I refuse! I can't! Who shut me up in here? John Paul, what have you done to me? I must get out. Run away. Already madness is creeping all over me. I feel it. Creeping upward. Yesterday it passed my belt, reached close to the heart. That's enough.

A car stops, its brakes screeching. The corridor is full of spiked boots. Why does he bother to protect me, to rescue me through his lock-jawed silence. A stray fragment . . . "Professor, what do you know about a foreigner by the name of Mordecai Neuberg?"

"Nothing, I haven't the slightest idea, I never saw such a man. I never heard such a name."

"And do you recognize such handwriting?"

"Yes, it's mine."

"And who's this same Dear Mordecai in the letter? Who is he? Huh? Who is he?! Who is he?!! Who?!!!"

John Paul, in the name of God, why? Is it at all

The Chocolate Deal

possible that the single justification for my existence is now your broken teeth, your palms turned to ashtrays?

"No, I don't recognize any such man. I never heard a name like that."

What are you guarding there? What are you sacrificing? And what's the reason you're left there in a pool? I must get out of here! Now's the time to test the heavy door and the stone walls, now's the time to climb up and gnaw the window bars or disguise myself as a bird and exit. I want to get out. This is topsy-turvy. What do I have here and whom do I have here? I'm not from here! I'm not one of them! Not wine, not coldness. Not darkness. I'm a stranger; I poison this house from the bottom up.

Now's the time to stand up and open the door and just go, take a direction east and head home and get drenched with rain and pierce the mist and leave tracks in the snow. Onward, right? Onward! In the likely direction. Once I approach the place, objects and the outline of the mountain range will help my memory. But I must walk by day and by night, forty days and forty nights on the strength of one meal, always walking. Oh, Hannah, I'm coming to you, they delayed me and it's not my fault. I'm coming. You recognize me. Despite the beard. I look like my father now, isn't it so? What can I do for you? I arrived late, but it will be easier now. It's hard to recognize me. I'm stronger. Before, I couldn't smash locks with a whack of the fist, split a wall with my brow.

How are you, Hannah?

I'm shrieking now, "Phillip! Phillip!"—because of the heavy key in his hand. "Why do you imprison me here? Out of pity? You're killing me. You're turning me into a madman!"

Phillip came. Brought me a bottle of wine from the last vintage. "You're hoarse," he told me. Exceedingly sour wine, dry, pale purple, transparent, and with two tastes—one you feel as soon as your lips touch the goblet, the other, the hidden one, reveals itself only after a while, like an accompanying melody. In the one was preserved the secret tradition of generation after generation of the best winegrowers; the other was the fruit of that miracle which emerges from a rather blind combination of indeterminable events. "The summer," he said, "was hot and dry, but touched by dew." As if he were presenting me with a bit of the secret behind all masterpieces.

So time passed. Phillip came back. Not saying a word, he sat down on a chair.

"What's happened?" I asked.

"They caught John Paul; they're interrogating him, giving him the third degree." Phillip was a quiet, matter-of-fact man, and only through a real effort could I make out the worry in that narrow face of his. "I know him. There's nothing to fear," he said, as though he were making a point. So why did I keep repeating the curt sentence: "I'd better leave."

"No," said Phillip. "Stay till the end."
"I'd better leave."
"You'll stay here. Nobody knows a thing."
"I'd better leave."
"Please, stay here."

Now he doesn't decide. Now he asks, the good man.

"I'm getting out of here."

He goes upstairs and comes down with two maps. One, a map of the immediate area. The other, a map of the continent and all its countries. Then he lights the wick of my lamp and spreads out the map of the continent.

"We're over here. The house isn't indicated on the map, of course, but this is the vicinity and here's the city. If you keep going southeast and cross the mountains, straight on, you'll finally get to the regions behind the war. There you'll rest," he tells me, "there you'll rest. Then go north, and follow in the tracks of the troops until you reach the place you left originally. There you'll meet, please God, your dear ones." Meaning, apparently, my mother, my father, Sarah and Rivka and Daniel and Hannah and all the others. That's his first mistake, but he continues to talk, about provisions for the journey in addition to the bread, the wine, the cheese, the dried fruits, the fur coat.

Suddenly he became very ceremonious and chattered, "The days are coming . . ."

I didn't hear the end of the sentence. Phillip seems pretty excited now. He says something like "The foxes have holes and the birds of the air have nests, but the son of man hath not where to lay his head."

"Enough, Phillip." I try. I didn't recognize him. He seemed inspired. Everything hidden in his heart these long years, everything treasured, breaks loose now. He must explain to me the great pain of a man like him, compelled to watch the sufferings of others. He must plant some faith in me, no matter how slight, that may stand me in good stead when I come to cross the snow-covered mountains in the distance. I couldn't stop him, even though these words of his frightened me. Though I was afraid my lonely outcry would return, that shriek which nothing in me can match. No, anything but that, and not now. What will he tell me now? "The days are now coming," he'll tell me, "when a man shall not hide in a cellar year after year from those who want his innocent life, and he shall no longer resemble a mole dwelling in the shadow of death." Nice words, Phillip, a sermon to silently rend the heart. And "the son of man hath not where to lay his head," and soon I'll have a place. There, in the mountains, high up, in the cracks I'll have a place. Way up. Nobody will know where I am. There I'll have a place. And from there I'll continue southeast, as you say. You're good. The brother of noble John Paul, and as dear as he. Just don't say anything now. Please, do me a favor.

"And what's on the other map?" I asked.

"Yes, the other map. Okay, listen, right here, not far away, ends the mountain range that descends west. There, in dark brown, the mountain wall rises. It's a region with few inhabitants or guards, partly covered with forests and rather thick wild growth. Where were we? It's already fall. Take along the coat and the warm clothes."

Now he takes a red pencil and marks out the best route he can estimate.

"I'll guide you to the last field of the last village. From there you'll be on your own. Take this two-days walk to the border in snatches, off and on. Move at night. It's now half-moon. Midway down the slope you circle a ruined fortress. Nobody's there, but take precautions. Go at night. Use the vegetation for camouflage. In the morning, there are caves in the area. Don't budge till the following night. The real troubles will begin later on, up there in the mountain passes. In the cold. But you'll make it."

He's right, no doubt. I'm strong. I cough, but I don't spit blood into my handkerchief.

"Who's there?"
"It's I, Sister Theresa."
"Please come in, Sister Theresa."
"I brought you some coffee and some slices of bread with margarine. You don't eat. You're sick."
"Thank you, Sister Theresa, I'm not sick. I'm healthy ... I feel fine."
"You don't eat. Why don't you eat?"
"I'll eat later."
"Aren't you hungry?"
"I'll eat later, Sister Theresa, I'll eat later."
"Your friend left."
"Yes."
"For a long while?"
"A few hours. He'll be back soon."
"Why not go outside for a bit."
"I'll go out. Soon. I'll go out."
"It's not good to be cooped up in a room all the time."

The Chocolate Deal

"I've done a lot of walking in the world. Now I'm taking a little rest."

"Good-by, Mr. Neuberg."

"Good-by, Sister Theresa, see you again, thank you."

Alone and lost, on the crossroad. You did well, Rubi, when you went away and let me go by myself, too—I'm through making one postponement after another, stealing freedom by the grace of chance, relying on the miracle of wrong choices. What have I accomplished that way? Those who hadn't the right to go on till now, now have the right, those who knew how to take advantage of their chances and make luck their own rule and habit. I, as you know, am not counted among these. I was studying troubadour poetry, and for a living I was a pretty successful journalist. I don't think I'm exaggerating when I say that I was on the verge of becoming part of the group of those sought out—at least for my professional experience. The number of worthwhile journalists among us has diminished considerably and those remaining are worth their weight in gold. The claim that I have an obligation to fight in order not to become one of the defeated has only a weak hold on me. I'm too smart and too tired to marshal the energies needed for going on. Now I'm quiet.

If only I had enough tumult in me to go to a strange woman, or to another city. In a ship I'd go over to one of the wonderful countries of immigration and change my name. If I were to make things easy for you... but I'm a burden for you. I've told you that more than once. Erase these words. I'm sparing you, in advance, any possible nights of regret. That's not a choice. It's not an act. I'm not doing a thing. It's a sort of silent, deliberate self-diminution, a kind of surrender to the vanishing point. I don't do a thing, I don't do a thing. I float, set upon wandering waters, set upon returning, crossing another region I was thrown out of, unnecessarily, at the expense of others, those who had futures, whose brows were iron to split things and whose nails knew how to take hold.

But this isn't a protest. Protests are addressed to someone. Don't imagine any bold movement against the powers above, don't attempt to hear a hand banging against a locked iron gate, or something of that sort. All that's going on here is nothing more than a silent diminution. I get weaker and weaker. Weaker and weaker. What deprives me of thundering voices and spoils my right to become another case of injustice or additional disgrace, is the element of obviousness in my situation. I've never suffered from megalomania, though I have valued my life. Therefore I don't exaggerate the importance of my departure. Whatever importance I may have is confined within these four walls.

It's no act. There's no need for any act at all. All there is to do in this case is nothing. I have no strength to refuse this peace, this great alienation. I'm here because nobody has seen me and I continue to be invisible. I don't contribute anything this way, and I don't steal anything this way. Any other conduct would force me to attach importance to my actions, and that would be a deliberate, foolish, wicked contribution equal to the huge senselessness all around me.

Lately my head constructs more and more conditional sentences: If only Moshko could take my place . . . Then, at least, I'd be spared this intolerable feeling of waste. All those who'd be the slightest bit pained by this death have made it easier for me already. I know that.

They told me. In the big building I was informed, when I came there after the mountain journey and the stealing through borders, following the tracks of the war northward, according to the good advice of Phillip, nourished by leftovers and refuse, getting leaner, wandering, carried by a maelstrom, in days when there is no King and every man does what is right in his own eyes, heading north, in the tracks of the confusion, the ashes, the soot. Seeing but unseen, and if seen—so what, okay, good, seen, then what, who has time to linger, wait a minute, wait a minute, what's this guy doing here, and who is he?

Now, the first trains pick up their pal-palpi-palpitating convalescence on temporary bridges made of iron or supported by thick tar-soaked wooden beams.

And spring is in the land. There isn't and there never was a spring like it for light and for the awakening of blossoms. I hear forgotten sounds; water, say, down a slope or wind in the leaves. Over there I hear a woman's voice and first laughter, and after it quiet.

At night, in a city whose name I forgot, men and women sat around fires, cooking soup. Children slept like exhausted angels on bedding of rags. Gypsies from the other end of the world beside a ruined castle. That happened not far from a city situated on the crossroad to the big city out of which the road climbs further up to our capital city, the first station on my return trip.

Clutching onto a train. Onward. Swift. Regular. Trained, experienced, grim, a shadow smeared on the roads, when necessary, penetrating, when necessary, walls that give an abundance of breeches and openings to wanderers like me.

A spring to please God. With many, too many to count, moving hither and thither, all meeting again in a whirlpool and breaking off and continuing on. And I haven't yet found an acquaintance, not even one, though according to my figuring I ought to find an acquaintance, if only one; how could it be possible any other way? A man walks in the street for about six months and doesn't meet an acquaintance. When did a man ever walk in the street for half a year without seeing an acquaintance?

What guides the birds across the ocean—the carrier pigeons? What's their sense of direction, huh, Rubi? What pilots them?

I was just now talking about birds. I won't say it was the same bird that visited my benefactor's narrow window, the bird that brought him the news with such loyal precision. (Poor John Paul's brother, where is he now, that professor of literature and salt of the earth?) It was this bird or another. It came to tell me something like: Move on to the big capital where the mysteries will be revealed. Where there's a tall building. And where you'll find a certain watchmaker. Or maybe I only imagined it. I reached the city and the tall building which, in its time, had served as a hospital for the community.

At the end of a week I found a few acquaintances there, the sort of distant acquaintance who needs a long while to remember you: "Wait a minute, wait a minute, you're what's his name, if I'm not mistaken, Yechiel Neuberg. The son of..."

I make the correction: "Mordecai Neuberg."

"Yes, of course! Mordecai Neuberg, Chayim Neuberg's son, no?"

There was, indeed, a watchmaker in the place. I remember this, even though I always used to see him from above, hunched over infinite parts in a fully lighted corner, with a watchmaker's monocle at one eye.

It's hard to imagine that about a century has passed since then. He looks at me now with his two empty eyes, like someone out of work, and murmurs the sort of murmur that's unambiguous but difficult to interpret. When I finally grope after something like—"You would advise me to go there and check personally, to see?"—he spares me the extra trip by nodding his head right and left, twice.

"It's not worth it?"

As before, twice. Just the essence.

"You're certain?"

His face drops and returns to normal. Twice. A wrecked information office. His friend is a cloth merchant in the old marketplace. I remember now. He had a small English clothshop by Santa Katrina Church. He gives me a look for a final

The Chocolate Deal

comment: Rely on him, it's not worth going back. He knows what he's saying.

That's it, more or less, dear Rubi. I tried. You saw. Didn't you?

Shechter, the watchmaker, will go on, so it seems to me. And Roth, too, the seller of fine cloth. His name's Roth, if I'm not mistaken. You, too. Not me. That's how it appears to me.

So I lived there in that tall building for about two months. They took care of me. Complete exhaustion, I guess. There were four floors and long corridors and many steps, glorious baroque style. After I recovered, they gave me a corner to rest my head in. A couch. In the evening the building was lit up like a giant hive, rife with movement and work: frying, laundering, buying and selling, asking and answering. Everything in a cloud of cigarette smoke. I'm sick. At night I hear them sigh, *cheh cheh*, talk in their sleep, and shriek all of a sudden. The movements of his face, watchmaker Shechter, my messenger, are still before me.

"Rely on him, if he talks." With great respect. And rightly so. Mr. Shechter is a wise man and a man of few words.

Once, toward morning, I got off my couch and, watching out for the group of sleepers, crossed the big room on my toes, like a man sneaking secretly away.

"Neuberg, where are you going?" I heard the watchmaker.
"Aren't you asleep?" I asked.
"No, I'm not asleep."
"Why aren't you asleep?"
"I can't sleep."
"I'll be right back; it's nothing."
He lay on his side, leaning on his right arm, as if he were reading for relaxation or as if he were some thorough supervisor who, tired from too long a sitting, allowed himself to stretch out a bit. He's considerably older than myself, as old as my father. Maybe that's the reason for that sound of supervision implicit in his hoarse, smoke-filled throat. It's not impossible that he's come a long way, that long ago he left all questions far behind. Once away from that realm of questions, he wanted to spare me a lot of time and extra effort, as if he were telling me: Listen, my son, to experience. That's all. But he didn't cry that day. I didn't either.
"What'll you do outside now; now where will you go?"
A woman's laugh was heard, strangled by a blanket or a palm. He looked at me. The faint light breaking through from the hall gave his face a special tranquillity typical of the meek or the meditative: What do you want? If I'm not mistaken he continued to say something, in his lan-

guage, about the wonders of living. Look, the appointed time's now fixed. This time next year. The woman laughs. The voice of a man is heard silencing her and a dialogue whispered far off. She lives on the third floor of couches. He must have thought I got up to move over to her there, by way of the suitcases. He knew she was taken. There was no bitterness in him at all. Personally he preferred these voices to the outcries of the bespectacled man: Faygele... Faygele... Daddy calling from the porch, toward evening, when it's getting dark and it's time to come home. Him they got rid of. Thank God. Faygele's sweet name died in the sick room. A clear case of madness. Where is he, and where is she?

If he meant the Faygele from our street, I'd remember his face. I guess it's a different man, the name's common. No? There was one Faygele among us, ten years old. She was the intelligent girl with a red ribbon. The clean girl. The talented girl who played endless études on the piano, shut up in her room, the beginnings of melodies wondrously lovely, heart-rending, toward evening usually, when a purple light paints the stone walls, when the bells announce evening and father is a dark figure in the street on his way home. Then, more than once, I thought I'd go mad if I didn't start out now on my own way. What will happen if I don't start out on my way?! But all this is kept inside the boundaries of sweetness. It's not so bad. Apparently, as it was explained to me, it's a question of age. At such hours we met to wander over to Nador's studio. The city soaring in twilight.

The watchmaker asked me, I recall, if I knew the woman who laughed. "I've seen her but I don't know her."

"You know her?"

No. He didn't know her. "A pretty girl," he said. "Go to sleep, Neuberg."

"What time is it?" I asked.

"I don't have a watch, but it's about three and still nighttime," answered the uncrowned King.

This watchmaker Shechter worries about me and I know it.

I have to get out of here. They don't keep an exact record. And in the end, who cares? At most two or three will wonder: Where's that Neuberg, what happened to him? What? Has he left? We haven't seen him. He disappeared two or three days ago and asked us to give his regards to Shechter. And Shechter listens and offers me one of his sighs, food for the road.

Where did I go? I went to meet someone. I wandered around for a few weeks, I measured

The Chocolate Deal

this filthy city end to end, a city that wipes its mouth like a whore, and I met you, Rubi.

Now I'm quiet. I go, apparently, to join up; by joining I acquire an address. I prevent my being pushed into confusion and into acts. No, there's no delayed surrender here, to those whose lips smile with self-satisfaction at this late going of mine. These people are sated, and they don't think such things, and soon they'll be gone altogether. We'll live in a city without enemies. I'm not important. So I'm deprived the sweetness of a perverted revenge, or the bitterness of a protest too hard to bear. If I disappear I won't make anybody happy, since all those who'd be hurt by it have gone away themselves. I'm no deserter. I find the right address.

The arena's empty. If I go into it, I'll be like a man coming with a different calendar to a new place. Time flies. You too don't lose a thing. The finishing line's close by. You'll be free to do as you please; that's the single offer I have in my hand for you. So poor am I.

The joy of dreaming is no longer mine. I cannot wager a thing on my future. I have no future.

When the other season comes for me, at the full end of so many years of sun and years of snow, I'll return to my troubadour poetry. Lo, she'll arise at the end of forty days. Arise from the water. I'll go ahead and dry my rough draft on one of the rocks of Ararat. I'll keep walking in the landscape that emerges washed, among dying fish and drifts swept into castles and schoolhouses.

I'll do as John Paul requested. I'll change my clothes, rest. Take the continental express up west. Come to his house. At first it will be hard to recognize me. Afterward he'll recognize me and weep: "Is it you, Neuberg?" "My best student" he called me.

"You told me to come back. You said if there'd be any reason to meet, we'd talk it over. Here I am, what do you think?"

Because of the boots that altered his face, I too shall find it difficult to recognize him. I imagine the housekeeper is pushing him about in a wheeled carriage, with a woolen blanket at his feet. She'll apologize: "Leave him alone, sir, he knows your name but it's better to leave him be. He's taken a punishment, you see. Because he refused to talk, he lost his power of memory. He won't recognize you, even if he smiles at you he won't recognize you. He's a very sick man; he certainly won't be able to help you finish your work. I was asked to refer everybody to Professor Tespiev."

Dear John Paul. How much of his suffering is my fault, and why does he bind me to him? What was the price of his silence and how does one repay him? If I were to complete my work and publish it at the university press, I'd dedicate my research to him, saying: "To the memory of J. P. Michlein, a dear scholar and an exceptional courageous man, the author dedicates his first fruits."

But I'm certain that by returning his soul to its Creator in the cellars of the third degree, John Paul undid the knot. I got this out of a newspaper that happened into my hands. In this way and not by a miracle did he turn things upside down. Now I'm freer. Right?

And details about Father are not known. A wise man, this Shechter, he gives out only the essentials. The rest I must guess at. How and when and where. That's how legends are born. I'm permitted to do as I please now, but neither doing nor done, Rubi, I told you, and so I simply become abandoned and stuck in the same place and I don't expect any shofar. That's how bad things are, just imagine!

Actually, I'd exchange all this constant trouble for a few strong Moshko years. But that's another conditional sentence. Lately these conditional sentences give me more and more of a sick stomach and it's getting worse. Close to death. Too bad. I haven't managed to visit the sun-drenched southern cities, to see the palms and the fountains. I haven't managed to love a woman.

*L*ESS BARGAINING than usual. Because it's too cold out, apparently. He hasn't enough ready cash with him. The rest he's prepared to pay with merchandise: a pack of excellent cigarettes, a tin of canned meat, a bar of chocolate, a drink of coffee. His hand is spread open before her eyes.

She turns, and he follows right after her. Closely. In the barely lighted snow, in the dark gray street. His hands in his pockets. Bent a bit. Two hundred meters. Left, and then another three hundred meters or so. And no words, no words, no words.

In order to guide him through the deep darkness of the corridor that exudes a mixture of mold, urine, carbon, and winter, she gives him her hand. A businesslike gesture that breaks his heart. And that's how they went up to the fifth floor. Then a door opens into a half-lit corridor, onto men's voices coming from the other side of each wall. And another door. And a room, two by three. She

The Chocolate Deal

lights a match and approaches an old-fashioned lamp redeemed from a forgotten pawnshop. She looks a bit younger now than she looked on the street. Thirty something, and not frightening. She says: "Let's have a warm drink." He places his portion on the old vanity table. She grants him the advance of a smile. Time to look her over. Something's there which brings to mind a quiet beauty without any tyranny at all. A kind face, like an unembittered memory. "Take off your coat." She's rid of hers. Then she goes over to light the coal stove. From her silhouette it's clear to him that he made a good deal.

He feels ice on his chest, as if he were on the threshold of a difficult obligation that will bind him to the woman kindling the coals, setting the pot on the fire. He has no choice, he's forced to take her into account. Not far from here sadness begins.

She does more than could be expected. The emerging interval between her movements and her half-sentences she fills with a warm silence, a soft trembling, as if she were known to him for years. It looks as though, in this narrow room, these movements become the heart of the matter. When she stoops at the foot of the bed and tugs at a can of coal-bits, he says to her, "Let me do it," so that, after a fragile fleeting refusal, she should let him do it. She goes to the curtains and makes a final adjustment. A closed fortress. She comes back and sprinkles a few drops of oil on the burning fire. There's time now, and suddenly the stillness is felt. Then she pours coffee into two china cups left there like the remains of a distant glory, and says, "This is the coffee you get nowadays." She breaks the chocolate he brought, saying, "Please, have some." "No, no," he thinks, "it's yours, in exchange for you." But it's too late, and that's too foolish. Meanwhile the stove keeps going. He imagines that it begs him to stay: It's cold out and late, don't go.

"Are you hungry? Do you want me to prepare you something?"

"No. Thanks. No."

But when did she become my wife, and what happened from then on? I'm tired, ready to fall asleep now on the bed. In my clothes. Sleep a little. Two or three jubilees. When did I last see you and what did you tell me? Not now. Maybe later.

And then he pulls out a pack of Admiral. What choice does he have? The quiet interval must be filled with something, gestures or smoke. "Please have one."

As something outside the account, a thank you in advance. With her long slender fingers she tears the cellophane wrapper. When he offers her a flaming match he discovers the true color of her eyes, that quiet, not yet ended dispute between gray and blue. Then he imagines that he's come by mistake to the wrong place. But it's hard to know now where and when the mistake began. She smokes along with him. That way she gives him back his privileges. Then he thinks something but forgets about it, in order not to put himself in too much danger. But it's impossible not to go to the window and adjust the dark cloth blinds and find out where he is and if it's actually so. It makes sense that this should be the city, now black, with a few lights here and there at the late hour. Turning his face, he sees her, sees her slightly bent back. It was amazing; she hadn't moved, hadn't budged from her place. Clearly all words were gone. The various movements refuse to fill up the silence.

She asks him: "More coffee?" A question which reaches him at the very last moment.

"No, thank you."

"The room's got hot, hasn't it?"

"Yes, it's got hot."

Then she leaves her place, puts the empty cups back in the sink, rinses them, dries her hands with a small towel. Afterward she approaches the bed. Sits there pensive for a minute. Wakes up. With the toe of her right foot she removes her left shoe, a small shoe that drops to the wooden floor, an object of beauty and pity. And now its mate rests beside it. She gets up, pulling the red bedspread. Folds it, with the help of her chin, in half and then in quarters. Places it on the empty chair. She undoes the back buttons of her silk blouse. Now she hesitates a moment. She draws out two hidden hairpins, and a waterfall of pure gold hair gushes down, gushes and gushes without a stop onto her bare shoulders. The skirt remains. Its turn comes, and down it goes. On the chair, its two colors, black and violet, sit quietly. She goes back to the bed and sits herself down, mounts one leg on the other and quietly peels off a silk stocking whose dark transparency unveils before his eyes an unbelievable purity. She repeats the act. Nonchalantly she gives to the movements of her hands a very ancient ceremonial beauty. A slanting line of a lighted foot, and further up, to a nebulous shadowy region, continuing on and getting lost in a forgotten land. God, I haven't done this in a long time. All bridges are burned now. Then she gathers up her legs and leans, all doubled up, on her right arm as if she were reading a book, and reminds him of an old picture now glimmering: I know you, but I don't remember.

Yes, I did my part. She's right. He approaches her and kneels by the made bed, resting his head.

The Chocolate Deal

But not for long. He knows now that her hand is playing on his head. From the sheet it rises up, that same distant eau de Cologne rises up to him. Her hand is frozen on the back of his neck. The time's come. It's clear to him that after many days this is really his hour. On the other side of no-man's land, approaching his private millennium. Then he realized that he wasn't robbed of everything, that he wasn't, he wasn't, no, and that he isn't the lonely object of pity that descends from above.

And now he's about to commit an act as ancient as death, which overcomes it. Therefore he disposes of his clothes and shoes, but his movements are sharper, more rapid. Then he pursues the only way. He takes this woman, and it's a unique moment of force and grace. He imagines that she was born thirty years ago only to wait for him, from then till now, deeply hoping, frozen in the corner of the street, and to lead him to her place, to these walls covered with paper flowers, and warm up a cup of coffee for him, as it was established long, long ago, and then quietly get undressed and wait for him. So he began to fulfill her hopes, to fulfill and to fulfill, lasting and lasting, a long while, unforgettably. To read on her face all that was happening to him through her, until he reaches for him and for her the limit; the limit? Until "an everlasting joy shall be upon their head," give or take a jubilee or two.

"What's your name?"
"Gerti."

Slowly, slowly the roads turn to meet. Time passes; that quack doctor gives a drug of forgetfulness to the hurt to quiet them and push them on further. It sends the lost to sleep the sleep that lasts and lasts till doomsday. An abyss opens between remembering and remembered, and that's where the rivers rush, that's where the year's seasons are, and that's where dark gray snow-covered cities are—cities, marble and gold from the sun. Kindled violet. And that's where the right of the wanderers is to defy silence, to dream, and go on.

"When did you see them?"
"I haven't seen them for some time."
"When?"
"I don't remember. It's been a long time. A long time."
"Don't hide anything from me."
"I'm not hiding a thing."
"Tell me."
"One day some men came and took them away."

The Chocolate Deal

"And from then on you haven't seen them?"
"From then on I haven't seen them."
"And you know nothing else?"
"No, nothing else. I knew nothing, nothing."
"And what happened to their house?"
"It was left closed for a while."
"And afterward?"
"Other people came to live in it."
"And you moved to another place?"
"I moved to another place, and then moved to another place, and then moved to another place, and then . . ."
"And you never went back to visit there?"
"No, from that time on I never went back to visit there."
"I want to go there."
"Don't go there."
"Why?"
"You won't find them there."
"I want to see the house."
"The house isn't there anymore."
"Demolished?"
"No, burned down."
"A long while ago?"
"No, a little while ago."
"Right. It was in the newspapers and on the radio. There was a little girl on the seventh floor. Didn't you hear about it?"

"No, I didn't."

"The firemen were afraid of the fire. Some unknown man there climbed up the ladder, all the way up, and jumped with the girl down to the rescue net stretched out in the street. Didn't you hear?"

"No. Why did he do it?"

"Who?"

"The man who climbed up."

"He must have wanted to rescue her."

"Was he her relative?"

"No."

"How do you know?"

"The papers said he was a refugee who just came into the city."

"He didn't know this girl?"

"I don't think so."

"Maybe he knew the house?"

"I don't know anything about that."

"It sounds like a dream."

"You're right."

"I don't know. Maybe he wanted the publicity. Some people are ready to do anything for publicity. I had a friend who studied at Rome University who bet he could stop traffic on the main street."

"What did he do?"

"He went up to the roof of the tallest building

in Piazza d'Espagna and there he did a handstand on the railing. A huge crowd gathered and traffic stopped. They wrote about him in the papers. They photographed him. I think the one who saved the girl wanted to become famous."

"Maybe."

"But they forgot about him."

"Yes."

"Maybe he did it for money."

"I don't understand."

"They wrote in the papers that he was a refugee. He must have been in terrible straits and told himself, I'll do something that will bring me honor and wealth—two things he certainly needed."

"Maybe."

"Seeing the fire approach the unknown girl, perhaps he did it out of pity, from pity or from an inability not to do it. At some moments the feeling of shame can all of a sudden be stronger than a fear of fire."

"But why did he have to be ashamed? He wasn't one of the firemen. Nobody there knew him. Nobody expected anything from him."

"It's not so rare for someone to jump into the water with his clothes on. Many see it happen. Among them there often is some unknown man who leaps after him in a matter of seconds."

"You're right. I once saw a scene like that, from a bridge."

"Did he know the suicide?"

"No, I don't think so. It happened toward evening, late; it was just getting dark. Before the very eyes of the people crossing the bridge, the man jumped into the water. A cry was heard, ho!—like that—and suddenly they saw a man jump in after him. The first man jumped feet first, as if he had collapsed and dropped by accident. The second man leaped head first, hands outstretched, like a swimmer."

"Did he pull him out?"

"Yes."

"Alive?"

"I don't know. A crowd gathered on the pier. Then a police car came and took him away. I think they took him to a hospital. There are always such lunatics."

"What lunatics?"

"Who jump down into water or climb up into fire."

"Do you know the doctor?"

"What doctor?"

"The girl's father."

"What girl?"

"The one who was rescued from the fire."

"What fire?"

"Do you know him?"

"Why do you ask?"

"Just like that."

"Which doctor do you mean?"

"The one who took Uncle Salomon's apartment."

"I don't know if he took it. I don't know. The apartment stood empty for about a week; then this doctor moved in."

"What kind of a doctor is he?"

"A skin doctor, I think."

"Mordi will be sorry."

"Who's Mordi?"

"My friend. I live with him in a cellar."

"Sorry, why?"

"He told me to send a letter before going to them. To wait for an answer. The letter just came back. He'll be sorry when he realizes that the Salomons are gone and have no other address. If they had a forwarding address, the letter would follow them and, in the end, find them. Sometimes letters get lost, for weeks and months, and sometimes even years upon years, until they find their way to the addressee. The envelope is covered with various post office seals and lines of red ink. Maybe the doctor knows something."

"What doctor?"

"The one who had their apartment after they left it."

"They didn't leave it."

"You said they left."

"I said they were taken away. I think the reason they gave no forwarding address was that they didn't know where they were being taken."

"You're right."

"It's already morning. I think I have to go."

"Where do you want to go?"

"I don't know. I think I'll go to Mordi and tell him all that you told me. But I don't have any time."

"Why don't you have any time?"

"Because I'm going to be rich."

"To be what?"

"Rich. To be rich."

"To be rich?"

"Yes, to be rich. Why not?"

"You could run over to your friend for a minute and tell him, and afterward get rich."

"Yes. But it's not so simple."

"Why?"

"Because he's likely to delay me. He's a good boy but he delays me. He always delays me. I came to this city a long time ago and only now you tell me the story. Last night, I was passing by in the street and I saw you. Do you always stand in the street on that spot, evening after evening?"

"No."

"What were you doing there yesterday?"

"I was doing nothing."

"You were waiting for someone. You were standing there as if you were waiting for someone."

"I was coming back from work."

"You work?"

"Yes."

"Where?"

"On a newspaper. In the editor's office."

"And finish at night?"

"I begin at three in the afternoon and finish at eleven."

"And what were you doing by the wall, in the street?"

"I stopped for a minute to fix my overshoe, and then you came over."

"Did you know who I was?"

"No, I didn't know then."

"Why did you take me to your place?"

"Because I liked you."

"Did it give you pleasure?"

"Yes."

"Was it ever any better before?"

"With my husband."

"You're divorced?"

"No.

"Where is he?"

"He was an officer. Killed in the war."

"It's already morning. I think I have to be going."
"Where?"
"I have to do something."
"It's early. Around here the offices don't open before nine. It's still dark out. And cold."
"Mordi will worry about me. I haven't seen him in years."
"He won't worry about you."

He gets up and goes to the window and pushes aside the heavy cloth just a bit. "You're right. It's still dark out. It's snowing." He goes back to bed and discovers, to his own surprise, how short is the way to her, how long her expectation. Again he is gripped by the special taste of Gerti.

He couldn't have guessed such an outcome in days gone by. At the end he hears something like —Oh, God!
"What time is it?"
"Twelve-thirty."
"I must go."
"I'll prepare you something; eat, then go. And I'll go too." She pulls out a loaf of black bread, cuts a few slices and spreads margarine. Then coffee.

Afterward they go downstairs to the dirty snow, to the dull gray day. They pass by gorgeous pal-

The Chocolate Deal

aces badly wounded, bandaged with wood and tin. They see forgotten iced-over bridges. They see green copper horsemen still drawing their swords, in praise of victory, to the leaden sky imposed upon the defeated city. They see Negroes in pressed khaki. Mongolians in boots and military tunics and fur hats. They see the dead who have come back to life. They don't see the living who have died. The city forgets fast. But the cracks that gape hint at their absence. Whoever seeks them stumbles upon bare trees, crooked alleys, royal boulevards, and their grim-eyed neighbors. He ends where he began.

Some say they themselves return to their city at night to terrify it with dreams. Some say they move about in it like a mute plea that wants to waken the heart against an unheard of abomination. They were natives of this city and gave it something exclusively their own—that spirit, that tremor, that sorrowful smile, that exquisite and sickly sharpness blended for their sake, dark-eyed ambassadors from a far kingdom. He thought about this when he saw how few black eyes there were among those coming and going.

Gerti wasn't thinking about this. She moves along at his side, guarding in her heart the joy of that right to pour another cup of coffee for this man who does with her as she pleases.

It was possible to end things. Right here. And from here on—that's the privilege of a solitary woman of her years. Sitting alone in the long winter: "I never had anything to do with such matters. What do they want from my life." Or something of this sort. Her gratitude toward this stranger, this unknown man back from far-off places, didn't mar her pride in her rare luxuries, luxuries discovered so intensely by the man who slept with her that she secretly felt certain he would come back to her when he remembered her, when he'd know what awaited him upon knocking once more at the door.

But he, walking quiet and remote alongside her, was certain. Mordi's all alone. What am I doing here? I have to retreat, get away before dawn, like a trespasser. Scandal. See, a window opens now and a voice calls out: Who's there? And another window, and a race of spiked soles on the surface of the empty cobblestone streets. Not to mention those dogs, strong-jawed hounds, that pinpoint his tracks in the clear snow and, at the high festive sound of the hunting horn, retrieve him in their mouths like a little bird to those hunting him down.

"I have to go back to Mordi."

But Gerti doesn't answer him and just keeps moving at his side, refusing to acknowledge his chance remarks. The third time the words are said like a declaration, screamed out over the terrifying groan of a massive bulldozer lifting a mass of debris from the snow-packed muck.

"I don't hear you," she hints. "Let's get away from here. What did you say?"

"I have to go back to Mordi."

"Why?"

"Because he's waiting for me."

"Is he a little boy?"

"No, but he's waiting for me."

"Send him a postcard; tell him you'll be back soon."

"It'll arrive after he gets the letter back from the Salomons."

"So what?"

"It'll hurt him and he'll look for me. He'll think I disappeared and start to search for me and search for me, and I'll never ever find him."

"Is that the way he is?"

"Yes."

Silence.

Yes. Yes. That's the way he is. So now I'll go back to his cemetery, go back to retreat the whole way. I'll knock on the heavy wooden door. Who's there? It's me—Rubi. Are you satisfied now?

Let's go die together. A shared sorrow is half a sorrow. I'll go to her. Good, then what? I'll go to her. I'll leap over his torso, over the cross of his outstretched arms. What'll I do there? I'll peel off her clothes. Good. And afterward? A second time. And a third time. How long; till when? Here's the dead guardian of my life. I was there with him in our story. In the hot steam of the handouts, among the other monsters. We had it good there, huh, just the two of us together, brotherhood of invalids, with no evil eye present. Enough for now. No, not enough. And no ear hears us foundlings here, and from here on we'll go and do something to glorify His Blessed Name and somehow our own name, and Mordi's there too, with a noble smile and with a cadaver stench exuding from his long thoughts, from his iron silences. And what was my sin? I went forth and reached Gerti, forth to another region. Inquire about my sin, huh? I evoked those sounds from her, so what and for what? Put Mordi between her and me, fine; there's Mordi who shall never forsake me. He'll stuff me with words. He won't rest. I want to go, to get out of there and wander. I won't go to him. That's that. All for you.

"I'm going to him and then I'll come back to you."
"If you go to him, you won't come back."
"I tell you I'll be back."
"You won't, you won't."
"I will."

"When?"

"Soon. This evening. Tomorrow. The day after. I'll just run over to have a look. He's weak. It's cold now. He's there by himself."

"And you'll stay there."

"To see how he is. Just to see how he is."

"How will you find the way back to me?"

"I know the street and the house."

"And if I won't be there?"

"I'll go and come back again. I'll knock on the door."

He knocks and silence greets him. At his back is something black and quiet. He turns his face and sees Sister Theresa: "Are you looking for him?"

"Where is he?"

"Two weeks ago."

"What about two weeks ago?"

"He died."

"Who died two weeks ago?"

"Your friend."

"Who told you?"

"I saw him."

"Wait a minute, no, really, don't cry. Where did you see him?"

"In the room."

"Hanging?"

"No."

"Poisoned?"

"No, not poison."

"Pistol?"

"No."

"How? How did he die?"

"I don't know. He was sitting by the table, holding a pen in his hand. I brought him coffee. He didn't budge."

"Maybe poison."

"Who knows?"

"You're sure he was dead. Maybe he was in a deep sleep. Maybe he was exhausted."

"They took him away."

"Who took him?"

"They came and took him. The doctor examined him and then they took him in a wagon."

"How did they know about it?"

"Sister Hedwiga went and told them."

"Where did they take him?"

"To the cemetery."

"Which cemetery? Why to the cemetery?"

"To the old cemetery."

"Where's the old cemetery?"

"Outside the city, on the way to the airport."

"... among those who shine like the bright firmament, the soul of Reb Mordecai, the son of Reb

The Chocolate Deal

Chayim, who went to his eternal home... because the entire congregation prays for the ascent of his soul..." Ten men, in black, and a cantor leading the way, praying, through mud and snow, behind the coffin. They stepped from the house that stands at the main entrance gate, circled the square along the bleak boulevards. "The Lord is my shepherd; I shall not want. He maketh me to lie down in green pastures: He leadeth me beside the still waters. He restoreth my soul..." So as to house him in a new lot, at the very edge of the field, far from the marble palaces and the polished blocks of granite. There were many a MAY HIS SOUL BE BOUND IN THE BOND OF LIFE over there, gold inscribed on stone, in square Hebrew letters. There were cold iron chains there marking the limits of family plots, for an eternal and everlasting honor, praise, and memory.

And here's Ludwig Hirsch, of saintly memory. Atop a china-and-crystal closet stands the picture of this dear man, in a black top hat, with a white beard that falls down his clothes like the beard of Elijah. A lovely beard, out of fashion now, the traditional length for other times. A good man who, amazingly enough, managed to divide his days between heaven and earth, with the help of God, of course, Who made all his ways successful and gave him a strong, gray brick house, a wife who was a fascinating woman, what with her pallor and gloom, and a loyal friend in whose big eyes was visible a righteousness inherited from the distant East and from a different blood. He dealt in lumber, I don't remember his exact business, and succeeded—why not? Hadn't he, all his life, done what was correct in the eyes of his Lord, not deviating to the right or the left? He read many books and dallied in mysteries, across from his alter ego, heavy and honored, who leaned on the mahogany table opposite the calendar and clock, a table brim full of business drawers and covered over with green velvet. Even so, he wasn't tight-fisted and got to see his name engraved in marble above the beds of the sick and in charity places and orphanages whose mute outrage fills the universe. He and his lovely aforementioned spouse, peace unto her, who rests beside him until the last trumpet, who gave him children (the mother of children is joyous): Karl, the first born, who was glad to take directly after his father; and poor Otto, that heartbreaker, who tried to hasten the Messiah's coming and preceded Him to distant Jerusalem; and Elizabeth, a gracious girl, who married a lawyer, Salomon, a proper, just, successful man; and Alfred who followed the exact sciences as far as he could, even to far away countries, to become a genius; and Peter, a rabbi in a community.

Snow falls on the Hirsches and their neighbors-for-generations, those whose luck was lucky and got a nice burial, whether city princes or city paupers, with their names engraved on white and reddish marble and on gray granite.

Now they're following after this unknown man, Reb Mordecai Neuberg. Amazingly enough, whether from habit or a sense of holiness, they continue to grant death its right to be respected and retailed.

I came here by mistake, says Rubi to himself. Someone led me astray. And nonetheless he came here to clear up the measure of truth in this fairy tale. The sun looks at him and says: "Now you come, sir?"

"I didn't know a thing. I was far away from here, very far."

"Go straight on to the square and turn left and then right along the boulevard. They're working there now. Ask for the one way in back."

In their tracks, erased and covered by snow, he goes along till he reaches the sign stuck in the yellowish dirt. He stands there for many days. Until the gravediggers come, tall and red-faced and blue-eyed, and tell him, "We're closing up, sir."

After quite a while they come back and tell him, "We're closing up, sir."

He looks and sees the darkness drop upon the city, and the lights of evening.

*T*HE REMAINING GYPSIES hang up their violins. The head waiters languish over the memories of the extinguishing Kingdom. The menus turn yellow as archive documents in spider-webbed cellars, at the close of the hopeless celebration. And just the tables with their white tablecloths wait around. The snow piles up. The iron eagles imitate the nauseating misery of a giant slaughtered bird. The skies fall on the sick city with incredible indifference. The evening starts early, its gray a jot brighter than the gray of those wounded towers jutting up with the absurd ambition of smooth stone ambassadors to the filthy, sticky heights.

But the noise expired, perished in the amounts of time accumulating into silence. How nice. So be it. Dark, curative. The war's all over.

Bad dreams stood on the doorsteps at the storm's end. The hostess of the house answers the knocking and drops down full length on the wooden floor, in a faint—is that the face of a monster? The far off shattering of china and crystal, sad elegant antiques.

In such situations the deep thinkers or comedians among the defeated tend to laugh weakly and end up coughing: We deserve it. Finally the military police intervene. Establish order. Hang a number of flea-bitten avengers, lovers of relics, men of excess virility. The shifting of military units commences on a wide scale and the dead, after their kind, don't sing God's praises.

More quickly than might be expected, someone bursts out laughing. A matter-of-fact recovery begins that demands a certain patience. Scarcely any are troubled by the problem of crime and punishment, with mousy thoughts of regret, so as to permit their neighbors time to get used to the new situation, allowing that it's hard to ask for more than that and what's done is done.

Afterward the trains return to schedule. The stationmasters come out again to stand in silence and salute. One blackout window after another is golden bright. And what's next? Next, a sort of Gerti, remembered in the last of her jewelry, standing opposite the mirror of the old chiffonier.

Then she puts dark make-up around her eyes, to look somewhat different. She keeps doing it. Where did we stop? Yes, there, then. So what will she do, say, to be more worthy? The pencil keeps softly underlining and passes her eyelashes in the direction of her temples and dies out somewhere along the way. For the sake of mystery. Tiring work. Now, in the heart of the mounting silence, among the faded walls, she quietly examines the meaning of the act. Beside her stands a chair with her dress and stockings on it, and chiffons in between. Silk. The room is flooded with the fragrance of a cheap-enough perfume, together with the odor of charred coal and winter and miserable pig fat rising up from the gray, damp inner courtyard and penetrating the latticed windows.

While she was sunk in that long ceremony, repeated and begun once again, who watched her? Many details remain unknown about him. It's known, though, that he married her years ago. The registering clerk and the priest established him as her husband from now to eternity. And that happened a short while before the Salomons were sent away.

"Officer," said Attorney Salomon to the officer who came to his house accompanied by three tall silent policemen, "there must be some misunderstanding here. I'm sure of it. Please allow me to make a telephone call."

The Chocolate Deal

"Afterward; you can telephone afterward."

Elizabeth, dry-eyed, packs something in a great hurry, something portable and valuable that stands in an inverse relationship to its weight and size, like a silver candlestick, a small pure-gold cigarette case, a wedding gift of jewelry.

And Yosie and Rosie?

They turn to Gerti, four eyes saying where to and why.

She doesn't know. What do they want from her life? Who am I and what am I? She now finds herself on the narrow boundary between the pursued and the pursuing, so it's better to keep quiet. Too bad. If she only had the permission to speak without putting herself in greater danger, she'd turn to that nice officer: "Please, sir, let him telephone, just telephone." That way it would be possible to dismiss that little misunderstanding created, all of a sudden, through a perplexing and rather frightful chain of events. Wait a minute, why? What's the matter? And so forth. As usual. But these guests, they had woolen uniforms and leather straps and boots and pistols and daggers.

"Please, Gerti," says Uncle Salomon, "take care of the house," and it's doubtful whether he's begging or using his last opportunity to speak on the strength of customary rights.

"Yes, sir."

The four guests now look very bored. It must be said in their favor that they don't cut short the rather lengthy ceremony. As a hint, the officer peeks at his watch.

"If they get in touch, if they inquire,"—he fixes his eyes on the guest—what should she say if they get in touch, if they inquire?—"please say, we took a short holiday."

Even though damp lachrymose November was there, with fallen leaves piled up in gardens.

Afterward, a few snatched parting words. Elizabeth cried.

And Uncle Salomon? Uncle Salomon only says, "Enough, Elizabeth, not now."

And Yosie and Rosie? Rosie hugged her mother's shoulder and Yosie finished locking the suitcase.

Watching from the porch, Gerti has a bird's-eye view: they enter the waiting truck. Now it tears off and goes its way.

Her long, pale, outstretched hand draws out a comb. Her hair obeys, keeps pouring down to her bare shoulder.

It's clear now that something will happen, that there's no other way. Oh, she puts purple, borrowed from an old celebration, on her lips. And, her heart going cold, she distinguishes another wrinkle imprinted to the left of her eye beneath the layer of ointment that was supposed to conciliate time for a while.

Yes, then she finds a job, more or less, on a respected newspaper that's rallying from its wounds this winter. She knows how to type, take shorthand, file, arrange, write memos. They wanted a recommendation from her former employer. That was hard to get. They took her for a trial period and were satisfied. She works afternoons and evenings. Goes home nights. On one of these nights, she stops for a moment in the street to fix her overshoes, by the wall. A stranger approaches, looks her over and suggests that he accompany her. He didn't remember her, and she was far from what he expected. She didn't know that according to the signs he gave, he had a right to her. He didn't remember her even though his memory was better than average. Perhaps on account of the distorted years, on account of the mixing in time of waters wildly streaming.

Many things vanished. The weak beatings of the heart remained. The sources. Luckily the sun kept its orbit, magnificently unconcerned. Therefore a few certainties endured, like the winds of heaven: East. West. North. South. Day and night. The seasons of the year. There was, in this, a sort of splendid abundance of mockery. What was left for him to do with the seasons of the year, or the winds of heaven? But the passing of time prompts the feeling of going from here to there. A few graced moments of half-crazed comfort: time is passing. And not in a circle. No. Anything but that. Anything but that.

But the number of acquaintances, or those of his kind, has quickly dwindled, and likewise the number of those able to give advice or answer a question. Not to mention the truly good, those who serve as your private wailing wall, as it were. Just listening, like that wall with cool cavities for the forehead, dark niches between one heavy stone and another.

The number of those no longer heard from or seen became so large that he imagines they were summoned heavenward. But his eyes see nothing that points to this, unlike the prophet Elisha he isn't equal to falling on the crossroads and seeing the fascinating departure of fiery chariots, that miraculous ascent, or something of that sort which would explain the many many disappearances, the letters going everywhere but never reaching their destinations, the weirdness of the one-way road.

One thing leads to another, to the illogical explanation that some giant, merciful sorcerer turned all the missing ones into stone so they wouldn't be marred by the fisticuffs of those unlike themselves. Not a bad idea, he whispers, guarding his secret. Oh, how numerous are your wonders, God! He earns a long peace that silences those of meager faith who envy him. Now he comes to his dim end. But look! The glorious resurrection of the dead is commencing. Time is amazed. Enough. Here are the sights of old, just what Ezekiel saw long ago, chariots and fire, enclosed by the deep of night. And the same magic tremor in the air. The next night, April is over; spring is nearby.

"There's another one moving around," said Corporal Jones.

"Grab him," whispered Captain Cohen.

*I*N ORDER TO EASE
the food shortage the authorities are now diverting to the market considerable amounts of surplus military chocolate. But it's questionable whether the chocolate is for eating or for cooking. Raw bulks wrapped in bright brown paper. Tasting slightly bitter. Primitive. The merchandise is packed in cartons one hundred by one hundred, carrying the seal of the armed forces. Rubi tastes some and finds it quite acceptable. Then, off and on, he sinks into long thoughts, the way great thinkers or inventors do who need solitude and silence for significant ideas to ripen inside them bit by bit, for the secret of some truth long sought after suddenly to become clear, like the green, ripping zigzag of lightning.

Yes, similar cases are known: the splendor of the treasured few, chosen by God, the sudden flickering of redemption.

But he doesn't finally call out in a loud voice: Eureka! Eureka! He goes looking for Mordi. Then he remembers that this time Mordi won't be able to help him as a confidant or adviser.

If I only had at least one person, if I could only tell somebody. Were Moshko by my side he'd light up an Admiral and keep quiet and weigh everything and say: "Not a bad idea, not a bad idea."

"Well."

"But they won't believe it."

"Why?"

"Because they won't listen."

"Why?"

"Because they don't know you. Who are you?"

"You're right. I didn't think about that. You're right.

"It's not simple."

"So now what?"

"You have to find someone whose professional authority casts out doubt and increases fear."

"You're right."

"A man who's willing to cooperate with you. And there's the rub, that's where you're stuck."

"Why?"

"Because he has to be someone known and respected and famous and trustworthy."

"Right."

"And a man like that won't cooperate with you."

"Right."

"That's it, friend."

"You're right."

"Because he won't want to risk his good name and get involved."

"And if he's guaranteed a share in the deal?"

"Even then he's likely to hesitate and weigh things and take a long time to decide, and he won't agree to stain himself for a doubtful profit. If you'd pay him his share at the outset, he'd see the matter differently, of course; he'd reserve a seat on the first plane out."

"I haven't a cent."

"I know."

"What do you suggest?"

"You have to make a commotion. Start a scandal."

"Right."

"If I understood you, you're interested in using this man twice."

"Right."

"Once to lower the prices and once to raise them."

"Right."

"And you have nothing to propose as an advance payment."

"I haven't a cent."

"But there are sparks in you. You're a genius."

"Thanks."

"Let's think, let's think for a moment. You have

to find weak points in the lives of those you need."

"I understand."

"In other words you force them to do something for you that will profit them."

"Why force them?"

"Because people have little faith, and most of them can't come up to the genius in you."

"Thanks."

"What scares them is the short interval between the danger and the profit."

"Right."

"And that's when you have to force them. Then they'll thank you. The only final judge is the result. I haven't had time to study many things, but I've managed to know people."

"Moshko, my dear friend."

"Stop it. Listen to me. You get to people through their weaknesses."

"I understand that."

"It's hard for me to tell you any more right this minute. The idea itself I like. Now everything depends on you and your ability to seduce. Surely you've seen with your own eyes how easy it is to deceive. Take a look at me, for example; I'm one of the deceived. Mortally deceived."

"Poor Moshko. When did they hang you?"

"Stop that. Listen to me. Look around for somebody who will pay attention to you. This city's full of people ready to pay for peace and quiet. It's a bloody city. Start a scandal with the help of those who want things to settle down, and pay them what they deserve. You'll get some money, and they'll come out with a double profit: money and quiet."

"I need the opinion of a doctor and the hired pen of a famous man."

"You'll find them. So long, Rubi. It'll be all right, you unacknowledged genius."

That's how it is, thinks Rubi. He walks under cold tar skies that turn the late hour into a sticky dough of silence and darkness. He could have been one of the King's advisers. Secret. Seeing but unseen.

And so the thirty days for Mordi who has no peace are over, the time of mourning for that poet who perished by mistake has ended for a while.

If I rent a room I'll be able to put in a table and set up a telephone on it, and a calendar and clock. And on the chair I'll be able to seat, let's say, Gerti. Something like: "Counseling," or "Export–Import."

The trouble is I have nothing now to pledge.

The Chocolate Deal

The disappearance of Uncle Salomon spoils my plans. I would have turned to him, asked for a short-term loan. Bought myself a suit. In clothes like these it's hard to conduct business with respectable people. They're bound to consider me a beggar and send their servants after me, or their dogs. The number of dogs in the city is increasing. I've had enough of running in the snow. These dogs, they have a rare ability to discriminate between the desirable and the undesirable, and until I convince them I'm one of the desirable they're likely to get terribly angry. I was sure I'd find Uncle Salomon here.

Poor Mordi, I was mad at him because he prevented the meeting for days and days. He knew the truth, or guessed it. When I'm rich I'll set up a beautiful tombstone on his grave. Dark stone and gold letters. A sentence in Hebrew.

But where will I sleep tonight? The hour is so late, there's none any later. I'll go to Gerti. Who will open up for me at night, in this damned everlasting winter? I'll go to the shelter house. I'll lie down beside them, beside those unfortunates who are as frightening as a curse, in order to hear them sigh, talk in their sleep, remember to shriek.

It's better to wander in the snow till dawn. If I go there, I'll catch a fatal disease. They'll take me out in a coffin. Drive me in a carriage. Lead me to

Mordi. In life and in death they were not parted. I'll go to Gerti. She won't open up now. She knows I'll never come back, that I'll follow after Mordi. She's taken in someone else, on the way, by the wall.

What can you do. Go to sleep. Go to sleep. All you need now is to roam around outside, to become a pillar of ice. If I could only disguise myself as something until . . . I have to get away from them, from this plague of misery, far far away, far far away, from the naphthaline blankets, from the mushroom and barley soup, from the righteousness visible in their eyes—see what they've done to me. I've heard it all before—you won't buttonhole me American style, you won't force me to take part as yet. I'm through.

Ah, here are the horsemen on their handsome horses, on their noble horses, their steeds that stand up on their hind legs. Here are the peerlessly handsome horsemen. And this is the street. And here are the foot soldiers. I know them personally. I know. They don't have horse stables and greased leather saddles and cold blades. But instead they have a cry always deep in their throats and blood in their eyes. And the horsemen are coming nearer, row after row. And there are our foot soldiers trying to grab those amazing horses, those horses of fame, by the neck, as if they were dreaming by the light of evening, as if they were trying to climb the Gates of God. But the horses shake them off their necks like a chance mistake and keep moving, and show them for the last time in their lives those tails that hang nice and long, the blue of their hooves, and keep moving, not thinking about them. And in the morning the city sanitation workers arrive. And rain comes to help them out.

I must escape. Look, the hounds that carried me in their teeth and brought me, a bitten gift, to their masters frozen in greased leather saddles are sleeping now. And now the horsemen too are sleeping a winter sleep beside their white, golden-haired wives, under woolen blankets. And the hunting horn is silent by the dimming hearth. Who'll blow it now. Who'll be mad enough to leave his bed in a night like this. I'll go away from here. I, the climber of ladders. I, the talented one. Professor Zultan remembers me. Prodigies aren't forgotten in a hurry. He, he's the very one who kissed my wise forehead after his yellow fingers had traveled, hastily, tremblingly, through my curls in front of Father's shivering chin: a favorite son.

Here's my hand, not frozen, its hollow upward, a hope for mercy. No. They lasted, my white fingers that bring to mind a pianist's fingers, that recall the movement of counting bills. Faster than the speed of thought. So I put myself in danger, so what? The police are now following up a scandal that's snowballing into a "chocolate scandal." "I'm not saying a word until I see my lawyer—Mr. Salomon."

Now for the happy meeting, long long postponed, with the dear uncle: "Your Honor, the Judge. He's my client..."

But things won't come to that. No. I haven't the airs to go through with the perfect crime. It's a regular deal like any other deal, without a single drop of blood. And what about those mouths gaping there in a terrible scream? A mistake, gentlemen! They're not screaming, God forbid. They're laughing. The hands supporting the belly, the tears in the eyes: "Good, isn't it?"

But where will I stay tonight? Tonight. The hour is so late. So so late. So. So. Late.

*T*HREE BANGS ON THE DOOR.
"Yes, sir?"
"Dr. Hoffman, please."
"The doctor's busy right now. Please wait."
"Thank you."
The waiting room.

The hundreds of cyclists who had to stop, alas, their traditional Tour de France competition during the bad years are on their way again now, at last, thank God. They're climbing the mountain. On the frosted-over roads among bare trees, a long caravan. And here they glide to the square of a festive provincial town. Most of them are stooped over, their bodies distorted in the last effort, while the leader, straight in his seat, lifts his right arm upward and rips the string.
    On the other side of the page he's covered with the kisses of his wife or girl friend. A good-looking man. Holding a milk bottle in his hand. In the

background is a giant picture of a man made of tires, alongside the apéritif Cinzano.

A giant purple-brown steak, crowned with fried potatoes and adorned with lettuce. Black Horse whiskey, the same good old whiskey, despite the upheavals of time, just like the Persian rugs and the bars of gold. Even the young girl opposite him still believes in Helena Rubenstein. Here she is, before our eyes, with her lovely smile, with her pure white teeth. Jamaican rum to add taste to the life of man. Incense from far-off islands. Mountain climbers wearing sunglasses, tied together by ropes, keep climbing higher, until, at the peak of peaks, there's nothing higher, just the cold winds of heaven. The Himalayan summit. By nature man aspires to get to the top. He's reminded of the story that makes the watchmakers laugh till they cry: Once every thousand years a distant bird comes down to peck one peck and no more into leaden Everest. When the mountain finally gives out, a moment of eternity shall pass, or something of that sort. A nice story just right for the ears of young girls, once their souls weaken, before they're separated from petite shoes, from their dresses. Ah, what a big and strange world.

Buy her a Doxa watch. The priestly hand of a maiden, adorned with a gold bracelet. The murderer from the blue forest is manacled. The city

The Chocolate Deal

breathes easy. Bitka chocolate, and likewise yogurt, good for long life.

"Please, sir."

And then he gets up and abandons the pile of illustrated magazines and steps after her. She's ahead of him and now she's behind him, on the other side of the silently locked door. Dr. Hoffman, the man himself, is writing out a cure in Latin. He doesn't sense a new presence. Then he blurts out, in the manner of the most important of busy men, "Please sit down." Then he lets out "Yes," a little that means a lot, something like "What's bothering you," or "What are you suffering from," or "What can I do for you," etc.

"I came to you, sir, to discuss the matter of surplus military chocolate that's streaming into the civilian market in large quantities."

"Yes."

He's listening.

"As far as I know this chocolate contains a tranquilizing ingredient that doesn't make it especially suitable for market conditions. With this gift of theirs, the authorities have shown a great deal of generosity. Even so, it seems to me we ought not to forget that this tranquilizing matter inserted into the chocolate is designed to pacify bold lonely men, on duty, young men torn from their houses

during the years of disaster, and taken far away."
"I didn't know about that."
"Now, sir, you know about it. Yes. Now you know about it and it's desirable for the general public to know about it too, through the publicity of a specialist's opinion."
"What for?" he asks, as if he doesn't understand or is pretending.
"So as to remove a stumbling block from before the blind."
"I won't do that." He girds himself with boldness. Just as was expected.
"Why?" I'm very quiet. I have time on my hands, in addition to the pistol, and my time is infinite.
"Because you're dreaming, sir. You need a hot meal, a new coat, a clean bed, a woman twice a week. You're taking unfair advantage of my patience and my weakness for fairy tales. I could have stopped you at your very first words and asked you to leave me alone. I'm a busy man, and many are in need of me."
Strong. Exactly as I was told, as expected.
"No, sir, you couldn't have stopped me at my first word, you couldn't have asked me to leave you alone."
That's how bad winds enter good houses.
"I don't understand."

And this time his voice trembled, as though a cold pistol were touching the back of his neck. Be quiet, sir, be quiet. Please.

"Because I'm the man to whom you owe your only daughter's life."

"I don't understand."

This time I believe him, and a further explanation is absolutely necessary.

"I'm the one who climbed all the way up the ladder to the seventh floor, in fire and smoke. I'm the one who reached her at the very last minute. I'm the one who grabbed her, pressed her to my chest with one hand while with the other I covered her with a heavy water-soaked blanket. I'm the one who jumped with her from high above to the outstretched firemen's net that, believe me, looked like a handkerchief. You were there. You remember. It's been a long time since then, but you remember, right?"

"You're the man?" He asks like a man made of chalk.

"Yes. I shaved off my beard and changed my clothes, that's why you didn't recognize me. You were shocked, nearly hysterical. You couldn't speak. It was just my luck and your luck that the good deed lasted an amazingly short while, the blinking of an eye, because if not, your daughter would've become an orphan on her way down.

Heart attack, a common thing in cases like these."
Nonetheless, Dr. Hoffman is still quite remote. Who'll believe him, he must be asking, without the corroboration of a laboratory test done in conjunction with the Office of Health.
"The news will spread. Via little birds."
"Yes."

He understands, or begins to understand. I can see it in his face. He falls asleep and wakes.
Let's go on, then: "In the heart of man nests a terrible fear of such pacifying material. In a western society it's entirely superfluous merchandise, how much more so in a society that has at present a real surplus of women. Because of the men ripped to pieces and by now belonging to a different earth for a long time."
"Yes."
"The prices will drop to zero. The wholesale warehouses will fill up with goods as movable as stones."
"Yes." That's all he says: "Yes. Yes."
"We'll buy all this chocolate."
"Who?"
"You, sir, and I." I guide him along my steps and clear up the obscurities.
"What will we do with it?" Amazement and naiveté.

"Then we'll see to it that these erroneous reports are denied. The starving market will breathe easy. There will be a rage of interest in chocolate buying. The prices will rise."

"Yes."

"We'll sell."

"Yes." He repeats, as aforementioned, "Yes, yes."

"We'll divide the profits. You'll fly to a new country. Far away. You'll build a palace for yourself, by a swan lake. You'll start a new chapter. You'll never see me again."

He comes over to me, saddened by the tie of friendship. "No doubt."

And what can I tell him now. "No doubt about it," I say. So I continue, at ease and off-hand. "That's why you didn't recognize me. You said you didn't know how you could repay me."

"And now you've come to collect the debt." Established too late. A very upright man, a bit shocked before an abomination.

"No, God forbid." And I really haven't come for that.

"If that's the case, why have you come now, after a long time? After such a long time?"

"I've come."

"Why have you come?" Now he's tortured by curiosity.

"I've come to propose a deal that suits you, that offers a profit just right for you and for me." Short and to the point. I'm not the cruel type. Not at all.

"You call it a suitable deal, you, the one who climbed up to save an unknown girl. By the way, why did you do it?" This time his question will sound quite pertinent to the discussion we're holding in clouds of smoke.

"I don't know." It's hard for me to answer that.

"You did it without knowing why you were doing it." He establishes and leaves a tiny space for the tone of a question that drags on feebly.

"I discussed this a lot with Mordi."

"Who's Mordi."

"A friend of mine who died some time ago."

"And he told you why you did it?"

"No, he didn't say. The matter caused him deep pain."

"What caused him pain? My daughter's rescue?"

"Yes." This time I merely say "Yes."

"What caused him pain? My daughter's rescue?" he repeats. Now he's quiet, left wondering over this amazing discussion. A cultured man, apparently. Mordi's opinion upsets him.

"Yes."

"Why? I don't understand." His curiosity, swelling, alters his face. He pushes aside papers and

The Chocolate Deal

flasks and turns to me like a relative. "I don't understand," he repeats, again and again, surmising the accomplished fact of some disaster.

From the adjoining room come the sounds of a piano.

When he's free, he sits down in the wide leather armchair, that refuge of peace and warmth amidst the heavy wooden furniture drenched with age and self-satisfaction, amidst dark oil paintings, a hazy saccharine beauty, villas and lakes and trees in mist. Through the window the dejected light of the dying day is smuggled in. He sees his twenty-year old head joined to Cathy's bright head. Forgotten pain. Since she left him, alas, before her time, he's had to turn to all kinds of other women.

That's not Cathy. That's Hannah. My sister!

Charlotte sits up straight at the piano, at the end of the carpet. The pleasing sounds of that fugue rush into the room, the same fugue of that very time, the day of the fire. A dear girl. His only daughter.

It's hard to figure Mordi out. He's a strange boy. Unpermissibly sensitive to those who are stubborn about living no matter what. I explain to him, to Hoffman, who Mordecai Neuberg is. He looks too much into things. Is that clear? I think this trait brought about his end. Right, he was a great burden to me. But now, without him, I seem to feel a weird lightness in myself. I think that's because I'm empty. He was a good boy. And I'm so solitary now.

"You loved him very much? You were attached to him?" He asks this quietly, deeply involved.

"We lived together a long while. You get attached."

This sentence has to end the first part of our conversation. Now silence again.

"Sir," says Hoffman, "will you have a drink?"
"Yes."
"Gerti, bring the bottle of Kirsch, please."
I see her coming near us, near us.
Obedience and respect. Now, right now, she identifies me as the man she must give her full attention to.
"Thank you."
Before I have time to think, the bottle stands between us and, beside it, two glasses on a silver tray. As if this Gerti were a magician.
"Even so, why did your friend disapprove of your good deed?"
He doesn't ask this like a father who must be grateful to me to his last day. He asks now out of curiosity, like a detached observer.

"I told you, I didn't always figure him out. My friend was a unique man, few are like him."

"And what did he say to you?"

"He made no pronouncements; he just thought aloud."

"And what did he say? Or, what did he think?"

Why does he now thirst to decipher Mordi's sad secrets?

"If I'm not mistaken . . . it's that, in his heart, he thought that an act like this which seems, and rightly so, the essence of beauty and generosity, a ray of significance, finally leaves behind a darkness sevenfold."

"I don't understand."

This time I believe him.

"At first I too found it difficult to get at what he meant. But I lived with him a long time in one cellar, in The Merciful Sisters Convent. What comprehension couldn't do, time did. His voice always in my ears, his voice that reminded me, not just once, of a bitter crying."

"Yes, you accomplished a deed that's good through and through."

"He claims there was a kind of betrayal in it."

"Do you smoke?"

"Yes."

"Please."

"Thanks."

"Betrayal?"
"Yes."
"Why?"
"A sort of atonement to it, a kind of amends."
"Atonement or betrayal?"
"A sort of atonement. There's something to his claim that my act of rescue, in this particular case, is the climax of a false play."
"A false play?"
"According to my friend Mordi, a false play is when you atone, in one moment, for the long crime against the many."

I'm telling him profound things, isn't that so? —profound and very interesting, because Mordi is speaking from my throat, dear Mordi, my dead comrade. I go on: "Try to understand him. He argues that if I had let your daughter burn..."

"Oh no, oh no." Twice he says these words.

"I'd have confirmed a certain practice."

That's the first hint. The doctor's face had frozen with the plea—Continue I want to know where you'll get to. That very moment his mute plea changes to—Stop for heaven's sake!

"According to Mordi, since I didn't let her die, the cry of the other girls is heard."

"What others?"

"All those in whose behalf nobody climbed up to the seventh floor. It's strange. I, who wanted to save your daughter from the fire, become in his eyes somebody who leaves those others on a balcony forever, before the eyes of the great crowd." Something of this sort I tell him.

"He's an interesting man."

"I told you. What appears to me as a personal protest, within the limits of my small capability, is for him an easy ugly way out. As a doctor you must be against this concept, since you doctors are always confronting individuals."

"You're right."

He's excited. He takes in my clumsy compliment with unconcealed pleasure. I can go on. "I know. That's why I told you he looks too much into things. In his eyes the darkness has now grown seven times darker."

"What does *now* mean?"

"My friend Mordi thinks that every good deed, when it's quite solitary, only points out the do-nothings, the stone hearts, the fools, not to mention the murderers or arsonists. 'In what way did the other girls sin, those who didn't merit a rescuing angel of the Rubi Krauss sort?' That's Mordi's sentence. I'm quoting."

"Who's Rubi Krauss?"

"I am. My name's Reuben Krauss, but my friends called me Rubi."

Now he ponders. Quietly. He's thinking and I don't want to disturb him.

When he's drowsing I ask him, "What's your daughter's name?"

"Charlotte. Why?"

"How old is she?"

"Ten. Why?"

"In another ten years, when she'll be twice her age, she'll marry some man."

"Yes. One day she'll marry. She'll leave me and go her own way."

"That'll be quite a celebration, nothing like it."

"Why do you say that." Again his face wears a mask of fear.

"An orchestra, many guests, and a fantastic amount of gifts, flowers."

"Naturally."

"I'll send her a bouquet of flowers."

"She'll be very happy. She hasn't forgotten the uncle who saved her. She asks me . . ."

"A bouquet of flaming roses I'll send her, with a short letter attached, saying: 'To dear Charlotte Hoffman, warm blessings on the day of your happiness. Reuben Krauss.' By the way, how many young girls never reached the canopy on account of you?"

Now's the time for a very long stillness. Dr. Hoffman lights a cigarette. He turns his face to me. "What do you know?"

"Everything."

"Who told you?"

The Chocolate Deal

"I was told, recently I was told."

"This is blackmail." Mute, mum, he ponders.

"To a certain extent. Yes, it comes to that."

Everything is out in the open now. Right. It's easier.

"I understand." His back to a wall.

"Don't be afraid, I won't ask this aloud. You'll make a proper marriage for your daughter. Far from here."

"And in return?"

"That you do all that I have asked. Who knows better than you the understandable fears of an average man about all kinds of sedatives. Men don't want to be calmed down. Just the opposite. They want to be bold and tense. Besides, this isn't the sort of tranquilizer that remains the intimate secret of one person. At best two know."

"I understand."

"After your denial gets published as a result of the misunderstanding, as the result of the error that always recurs, a stone drops from the heart. No one will accuse you. The prices rise, and rightly so. You take what's yours and go far away, if that's what you want, and make a suitable match for your daughter. At most you adopt a new name, southwestern, hot and gay, with a nice sound to it."

"I understand."

"That way you remove from yourself, in advance, any additional troubles."

"I don't understand."

"I want to kill you. I haven't yet made up my mind against the idea. Maybe I'll do it. I think I'll soon kill you."

"You won't, Mr. Krauss. Tell me you've changed your mind about it. You only said it in fun."

"Okay, I won't kill you. I have to go now. Your waiting room is full to the brim."

His Gerti opens the door for me.

No. This is the center of the continent stiffened by frost, white under black skies, soaked in smoke and soot. Let us go now and wait for the inevitable. Here's the sadness of the little victory. Let's wail a bit. No, no. Let's just go. It's not late yet. We'll measure the streets. Afterward we'll decide something, at least we'll decide where we'll sleep tonight and what we'll do tomorrow. Tomorrow or the day after the clamor will begin, the terrible scandal will burst. And I have nobody to share my story with. Mordi's gone, and lately I haven't seen Gerti. Mordi will smile and say, "Okay, so what?" He won't tie a laurel wreath around my head, in the name of brotherly love. "Okay, so what?" It's true I'm not reforming the world. They're reforming it without me.

The Chocolate Deal

Here, for instance, right here, not far away, opposite a wall of boards closing off a contaminated area, with cracks to peep through onto extensive public works. You can see the hovering flicker of blue soldering lights. You can hear a heavy hammer beating, iron on iron. Enough. Stop. And in the icy silence a man's voice is clearly heard: "Heave it higher! Heave!! That's the way! Wonderful! Excellent!" A giant crane stands there. A monster. Now they're attaching something. Soon will be heard the groan of those pulling it up and up, hauling it out of the water. "A little to the left! A little to the left!"

I'm hungry. What time is it? According to the tower, eight-twenty. To Gerti. But it's too early. She finishes between ten and midnight. Who knows where she is now. She must have moved off to another place. She's not sold to me forever, but always unknown in advance. I can only make a quick guess about her. What do I know. I don't know a thing. Who can count the number of her needy on earth. A good girl who manages to adjust to the great things, the mysteries. She has a room, but no voices reach there, and in that room a weak fixed amount of light and a bed lying at the ends of this city, at the tag end of time, always. There she can warm up for me the eternal cup of coffee of the innocent. She's perfect. Unscratched. With that frightening earthy immediacy and the ability to blush on hearing compliments. Except for her darknesses, what do I know about her?

Then he freezes. White. She didn't reveal to him the one or two missing links, her being Hoffman's secretary now, Salomon's heir, heir to the house, to the furniture, this woman. How come he didn't feel her presence as she opened the door for him, how come he didn't catch the grimace of surprise on her face. But this is some other Gerti. The sameness of the names misleads me toward the quiet outrage jailed in my sick brain. No, there's no connection, no connection whatsoever. This other's older and grayer. I'm too tired.

I need Gerti, in addition to all the other reasons, for her connection with the newspaper and its journalists. If Mordi were alive, he'd help me. He was a poet, though he made his living and his name as a journalist. He'd prepare a report for me on the chocolate matter which would have the power and magic of shock. He'd throw himself and me into the joy of the act. He'd show them who he was, what sort of a giant was hiding inside his sorrowful figure. But he preferred to fade away.

When the day comes, I'll set up a tombstone on his grave, a beautiful one, dark brown, engraved

The Chocolate Deal

with gold letters. Hebrew. I need him so badly. What'll I do? It's winter now. I remember a summer on park benches. Mordi and me, there. At night. Soon we'll get to our cellar, I'll be able to write to my Salomons. I had the patience to wait and he hadn't the strength left to go on. One day they'll ask me: "What did Mordi actually die of?" Who knows? Some distant relative will wander the length of those years, will piece together the details: they last saw him with a certain Rubi Krauss. They'll tell him: they lived together in a cellar in the courtyard of a certain convent, they were often seen together in the community soup kitchen. But nobody knows where that particular individual is now. They say he made a success on the black market and collected a pile of money and beat it for Venezuela. An oil deal. They last saw him at the Caracas Casino accompanied by his new mistress.

What will I tell his relative if he asks me: "Mr. Krauss, what did Mordi die of?" I don't know. Rumor has it that he left a letter behind. Rumor has it. Rumor has it. I don't know a thing, what do you want from me. I begged him to join me, so we'd get out together, and go far away. He didn't want to go. He wanted to stay. And maybe he was unable to move anymore, to roam. Left on one spot, at one time, like the dial-hand of the clock on the city tower that holds forever the earthquake second of its destruction.

"They say he left you a letter."

"No, sir, he left me no letter. Maybe he wrote one and burned it. I don't know."

"Did he hang himself?"

"They told me he didn't. They said they found him seated at the table as if he were napping. That's what they told me."

"Maybe he took poison?"

"No. He didn't take poison. He didn't need any. Maybe he went to take Moshko's place."

"Who's this Moshko?"

"A friend of ours."

"Why take his place?"

"In order to prevent too great a feeling of waste, in his opinion, in order to win Hannah."

"I don't understand."

"It's hard to understand."

"I don't understand."

"I say it's hard to understand because such things are best done in darkness, and modesty's good for them, as they say."

"And this Moshko agreed to it?"

"Moshko is hanging from the tree."

"And who's this Hannah?"

"My sister. I had one sister and her name was Hannah. Mordi loved her all his life."

The Chocolate Deal

The man will go away and pity me, or leave in a hurry, frightened. I didn't invite him. What could I tell him? Everything was true to the core. He'll take me for an idiot. An unfortunate relative following Mordi's footsteps.

*A*H, the newspapers shall leap to the subject: bold race horses, mad to gallop, torn loose from their halters. The radio too shall do its best. And the city shall celebrate one of its most amazing nightmares.

When Dr. Hoffman shall be called in to give his opinion on the matter, he'll say something like: "We have reason to believe that this military chocolate contains very strong tranquilizing material whose effect lasts from two days to a week, though it cannot be tasted. At this stage it's hard for me to say more."

These hinting remarks shall strike terror into the wholesalers. They'll hurry to deny the report altogether. Their denials shall turn the community into a terrified, enraged animal. A spokesman from the supplies division of the temporary garrison shall laugh out loud: "Our boys keep chewing this chocolate and it looks to me as if I wouldn't be wrong in saying they don't seem, God

The Chocolate Deal

forbid, very calmed down." He'll try to furnish additional proof, then give it up.

But in an atmosphere of suspicion, typical of twilight times between one age and the next, these clear words won't stay the stormy winds. Experienced people shall say to each other: "There's no smoke without fire," or "Denials are affirmations of the denied."

Rubi, standing by, shall see how the prices drop from hour to hour. The picture of disaster: the chocolate shall fill the warehouses "like immovable stones." At a certain moment the merchants shall say, in their broken hearts: "Let's pay somebody to hire porters to clear out these mountains."

Then Rubi shall go outside, along the streets of the confused city, to that place. That very day he shall purchase ten tons of merchandise, packed in big cartons, paying only what it would cost to hire porters to get rid of this chocolate, and load it quickly onto three big trucks.

The transaction won't have the noise and the light and the laughter characteristic of public auctions in the square. With no other buyer, the deal shall be snappy and to the point. Outside, the round winter sun shall stand like a purple ball in the dark clotted skies, and the odor of burning coal shall be stiff in the air, mixed up with the heavy food of this part of the continent.

Afterward the tide shall turn back, as was foretold and foreseen. The vain fears shall vanish like smoke. Mistakes can be corrected. The prices shall rise. The city shall laugh like mad for two days and quiet down. The retailers shall rejoice, and the customers too.

Rubi shall remember Dr. Hoffman and his great kindness. He will not kill him. He will also recall Gerti, who helped him in his days of indigence to open the door to the business world.

"Rubi," she'll say to him, "I know you're an honest man. One day you'll pay me back."

And he shall repay her with minks, with giant diamonds, and with a Jaguar, with rare white wines, with marble hotels surrounded by palms, with rich steaks, with Yemenite coffee strong as legend has it, with cream cakes.

From there he shall go to the old cemetery and set up a tombstone on Mordecai Neuberg's grave. A high granite column, lovely and dark and engraved in gold.

The *Chocolate* Deal

The last ones to leave the cemetery saw, as evening fell, a man kneeling, in tears, endlessly crying and drying his face with his torn sleeve, and finally falling asleep.

When he awoke he saw a stranger come toward him and say: "Are you Mr. Reuben Krauss?"

"Yes."

"Mr. Shechter is looking for you."

About the Author

Haim Gouri is a multifaceted poet and writer who resists categorization and draws on many and varied sources. His achievement has been to transmit these influences into a body of work that is original and coherent. Gouri's use of modern Hebrew commands a full range of tones, from self-mockery to romantic and erotic, from elegiac sadness to heroic celebration, from elegant simplicity to the layered influences of biblical, Mishnaic, talmudic, and medieval Hebrew in the pursuit of a modern poetic idiom.

Haim Gouri was born in Tel Aviv in 1923, attended the famous Kaduri Agricultural High School, and upon graduation in 1941 joined the Palmach, the elite commando units of the Haganah, the forerunner of the Israel Defense Forces. In 1947 Gouri was sent to Europe to help Jewish refugees who survived the Nazi Holocaust, an experience that has had a deep impact on his creative endeavors. He returned from Europe to fight in the war for Israel's independence in

1948–49. After the war, Gouri studied Hebrew literature, philosophy, and French culture at the Hebrew University of Jerusalem. He received his B.A. with honors in 1953 and spent the following year at the Sorbonne in Paris studying contemporary French literature.

As a poet, journalist, novelist, and documentary filmmaker, Gouri's work reflects Israel's political and cultural transitions. In 1961 he covered the Eichmann trial for the Hebrew daily, *Lamerhav.* In the 1970s and 1980s he wrote and produced *The Eighty-First Blow, The Last Sea,* and *Flames in the Ashes,* a trilogy of films on the Holocaust, the "illegal" immigration of Jewish refugees to British Mandatory Palestine, and the Jewish resistance to the Nazis.

Gouri has published twenty-two books, including twelve volumes of poetry and ten works of fiction, essays, and journalistic reportage. His works enjoy great popularity in Israel, and many of his poems have become part of the nation's cultural canon. An honorary member of the Academy of the Hebrew Language, Gouri is the recipient of Israel's top literary and journalistic prizes, including the Bialik Prize (1975), the Israel Prize for Poetry (1988), and most recently, the Uri Zvi Greenberg Award for Poetry (1998).